THE ROCK BOYZ

Money, Power & Respect

TWYLA T.   PATRICE BALARK
DANI LITTLEPAGE   J. DOMINIQUE

The Roc Boyz: Money. Power. Respect.

❀ Created with Vellum

This series is dedicated to our wonderful supporters! If it wasn't for you all, we would be reading our own work. Thanks for supporting us!!

DISCLAIMER

You don't have to read the Thug Holiday series to enjoy this one. The guys were included, but you didn't know their point of view. You'll get that in this book and if you want to read about the Holiday Sisters, feel free to do so after you finish this book. For those of you who have been following the Thug Holiday series, we have added the last four chapters just for you. Happy Reading Loves!!

✊ I ✊

J.R. took a hard pull from the backwood he was smoking before tilting his head back and blowing out the smoke. He had been robbing and killing niggaz since he was fifteen and never been shot at until that night. He would be lying if he said that the shit didn't have him fucked up in the head but actually showing it would never happen.

"So, nigga, you care to explain what the fuck happened back there?" D'Mani asked calmly, flaming up a blunt of his own.

"Look... like I told y'all niggaz back there, don't worry about it, I got this," J.R. replied, locking eyes with him from the opposite side of the table.

"DON'T WORRY ABOUT IT? MY WIFE WAS ALMOST CAUGHT UP IN THAT BULLSHIT!" D'Mani's twin brother D'Mari barked before pounding his fist on the table and standing to his feet.

Blame it on natural reflexes because before anybody could blink, J.R. too was on his feet, except his hand was placed on the pistol that was at his waist.

1

"Look, everybody needs to calm the fuck down. We not gon' get shit resolved doing all this unnecessary bullshit. J.R., you put all of us in danger, including our women and your own. Now if you know something then you need to tell us something. This ain't our city, this yo shit... and if moving here from New York is going to place us in some drama because we are affiliated with you, then we need to know what's going on," Corey spoke, easing the tension in the room momentarily.

Silence fell upon the four men before J.R. began to speak. Although he hadn't contemplated long about it, he knew he could trust the men in front of him with his life, so he explained.

"About six months ago, my homie Rio switched up on me. We been making moves together since we were shorties. Unbeknownst to me, the motherfucker was working with the FEDS. Now, although he never gave me up, he snitched on our plug, Tessa. He knew me and Rio ran together so because Rio is in protective custody, he sending niggaz at me. I look at the situation like this, since he already started a war, I might as well prepare myself to battle. I'm a one-man army in these streets, and as you can tell from the Rio situation, trusting niggaz is not on my to-do list, so I'm out here solo," J.R. explained.

D'Mani, D'Mari, and Corey all looked at him as if each of them was in deep thought. J.R. knew his beef with Tessa's cartel was going to explode; he just had no idea it would happen the opening night of his girlfriend's club. He felt like shit for putting them in danger, but at that point, he needed to dead the shit before someone close to him got hurt.

"What type of product is Tessa moving?" D'Mani quizzed.

"Pure white. He's the distributor for half of Georgia," J.R. replied.

"How's his team?" D'Mari questioned next.

"Mediocre like a muthafucka, that's why I ain't been tripping. Them niggaz can be touched... it's just taking time cuz I'm a one-man army."

"So, what's ya plan?" Corey chimed in.

"Get money, that's always the plan," J.R. shrugged.

"Aye look right, money in New York is cool or whatnot but honestly, we came to Atlanta to expand our business. We got our team there and shit is running smoothly, if we can...."

"Can what? I thought the plan was to get out the game," D'Mari cut his brother off in mid-sentence.

"Nigga, it is but..... you trying to retire now and be broke in seven years? Think about it, we take over here, do you know how many more opportunities and doors that would open up to us? I'm trying to make sure my family straight forever, just not the time being," D'Mani advised.

J.R. was feeling everything Mani was spitting. He hadn't known them long, but he knew how they moved. They were the husbands and boyfriend of his girl's sisters so trusting them came slightly easier.

"I gotta admit, that don't sound like a bad idea," Corey shockingly stated.

Just as J.R. was about to speak, he heard his name being called from upstairs. He took a deep breath because he could tell by the tone in Lexi's voice, she wasn't happy.

"Y'all sit here and think about this shit. Let me go talk to this girl." He announced, standing to his feet and heading up the stairs.

As soon as J.R. stepped foot in the kitchen, all eyes were on him as the Holiday sisters stared a hole through his soul.

"What's up baby?" he asked, locking eyes with his girl.

"You motherfuckers down there talking a lot, yet neither one of you musty fucks came up here to tell us anything," Lexi snapped.

"Look, Lexi, shit is being handled," he replied, turning to walk away.

"HANDLED? We were just shot at, at the opening on my club, what type of shit is that?" she yelled.

"Yeah bro, like for real, we need answers," Lexi's oldest sister Drea chimed in.

"I know sis but the less y'all know, the better. We got shit under control. What happened tonight will never happen again... y'all got my word."

The Holiday sisters were cut from a different cloth. They weren't from the hood and had never been exposed to it until they started dealing with their men. J.R. snagged Lexi a year ago when she was in her last year of college at Clark. She was dancing at a club there to support her expensive habits. At first, J.R. was cool with that until he fell in love with the youngest Holiday sister. It wasn't long before he made her quit. As a graduation gift to her, he bought her a strip club of her own and now she was pregnant with their first child.

"I love you baby, but you gotta trust me," J.R. said, walking over to her rubbing her small stomach and kissing her on the cheek.

J.R grabbed a bottle of water, ignoring the stares from his sister-in- laws and headed back down stairs. He knew they were shaken up, but there was no time to dwell on the past when there was moves to be made.

"You good homie?" D'Mari asked once he reentered the basement.

"Yeah but y'all niggaz gon' have to explain this shit to y'all women when y'all get to the crib," he replied.

"Ain't that a bitch. We gotta explain and the shit ain't have nothing to do with us," Corey barked, but J.R. ignored him and lit another blunt.

"So, what y'all wanna do?" he asked but quickly raised a finger in the air silencing them.

He heard the floor creek over his head and had a feeling that the sisters were eavesdropping. So, he grabbed the remote control to the stereo and turned it on.

"So what y'all wanna do?" J.R. asked again before the music started blasting through the surround sound.

The four men sat quietly, weighing their options.

"I wanna get this money," D'Mani spoke, pouring a shot of Henny into his glass.

"Money, it is," Mari followed behind him, pouring a shot of his own.

"Say less," was all Corey said as he took the Henny bottle from Mari and tossed it back straight out the bottle.

"To getting this money."

J.R. raised his glass in the air and the boys followed suit just as the music blared.

> ♬*And the winner is Hov, my man, speech!*
> *First of all I wan' thank my connect*
> *The most important person with all due respect*
> *Thanks for to duffle bag, the brown paper bag*
> *The Nike shoe box for holding all this cash*
> *Boys in blue who put greed before the badge*
> *The first pusher whoever made the stash*
> *The Roc Boys in the building tonight*
> *Oh what a feeling I'm feeling life* ♬

The lyrics to Jay Z's song *"Roc Boys"* serenaded their ears as they listened to the lyrics attentively.

> ♬*The Roc Boys in the building tonight*
> *Oh what a feeling, I'm feeling life*
> *You don't even gotta bring ya paper out*
> *We the dope boys of the year, drinks is on the house*
> *The Roc Boys in the building tonight*

TWYLA T.

> *Look at how I'm chilling, I'm killing this ice*
> *You don't even gotta bring ya purses out*
> *We the dope boys of the year, drinks is on the house* ♫

"To the dope boys of the year," J.R. yelled over the music.

"To the Rock Boyz," the four of them said in unison, putting a stamp on their new beginnings.

6

2

"Ummm... aww shit! Right there baby... oooh I'm bout... I'm bout to cuummm!"

D'Mari was fucking the shit out of Drea and her shit talking only turned him on that much more. When he felt Drea's legs shaking, he felt her liquids flowing simultaneously. She was wet as fuck and that sent him over the edge.

"Boy why you didn't pull out?" Drea fussed after Mari fell down on her.

"Pussy too good," he chuckled and she playfully hit him.

"I ain't tryna get pregnant. We got two little ones and that's enough."

"If it happens, it happens," he told Drea as he got up.

"You a damn lie!" He heard her huff as he made his way to the bathroom.

Drea said that she was fine with just Ava and DJ, but D'Mari didn't mind having a big family. He turned on the shower and then brushed his teeth and washed his face after taking a piss. As soon as Mari stepped into the shower, Drea came into the bathroom and stepped in with him. They washed each other off. Mari tried to pin her up against the wall, but she playfully swatted his hand away.

"Woman that's *my* pussy, you can't deny me."

"I have a meeting at nine and you woke up messing wit me," she laughed.

"I got a meeting too, so Ima let you make it," he smirked.

They finished washing each other off and got out of the shower and dried off. D'Mari was set to meet with some investors, and he needed the shit to go well. When he transitioned from New York, he really thought that he was putting himself in position to retire from the game; but it appeared that wasn't happening and the street shit was just meant to be. However, he had to ensure that they had enough legal businesses to clean the money up since they planned on taking over the streets of ATL. D'Mari got dressed in a black Armani suit, brushed his waves, kissed Drea and the twin's goodbye, and then headed out. Mari hoped in his Audi since it wasn't in the garage and headed out. About ten minutes into the drive, Mari's phone rang and it automatically connected to the Bluetooth after a few seconds.

"What up?"

"What up cuz? You on the way?" Corey quizzed.

"Yes sir... everything still in place right?" Mari asked.

"Yep, but you sure you don't want me to meet you there? Just in case. It ain't like we know these niggaz and you meeting at their place."

"Just handle the other business. I got this. It's just a meeting."

D'Mari chopped it up with Corey for a few more minutes and then hung up. The sounds of Tupac filled his car after the call ended and Mari rapped along with him. No matter what, Pac would be his all-time favorite rapper. Most New York niggaz rolled with Biggie just because, but Mari always went against the grain. He liked them both, but if he had to

8

choose, Pac would always be his choice. Thirty minutes later, Mari made it to his destination and parked. Traffic was a bitch in Georgia and no matter what time you left, you were bound to get caught up some kinda way. There was always an accident somewhere because of non-driving mu'fuckas, but Mari tried not to complain because it was really worse in New York. D'Mari was still in disbelief that he was a married man, but he wasn't complaining. After all, he was married to one of the Holiday sisters who happened to be a lawyer. Andrea didn't know the ins and outs of what all he did, and he hoped that she would never have to know any details. The less she knew the better.

He grabbed his briefcase, checked for his other shit, and then got out. Mari walked inside and was greeted by a red head, blue eyed receptionist. He wasn't expecting that shit at all because when he called the day before, the receptionist sounded black as hell. Mari figured that maybe it wasn't the same girl; but when he made it to the desk, he saw her name tag and when she spoke, he knew that it was. He knew that she was definitely fuckin' one of the Harold brothers; but that wasn't his business at all, and he didn't give a fuck.

"Good morning, Mr. Mitchell. Mr. Harold will be with you soon," she motioned for him to have a seat.

Mari copped a seat and impatiently waited for Jason to hurry the hell up. He couldn't lie and say that he wasn't feeling some type of way because he was a prompt nigga and made it fifteen minutes early. Mari pulled his phone out and noticed that it was currently twenty minutes after nine. A text came through from Corey, but he heard Jason's voice before he could open the text, so he decided that he would wait.

"Mr. Mitchell... come on back!"

D'Mari stood and made his way down the hall right behind Jason. He had never met with buddy before, but

Corey had. D'Mari was the business and mastermind of the crew, but they all agreed to do whatever was necessary to make sure shit ran amongst the crew. As D'Mari looked around more, he began to think that The Harold's should have been propositioning them and not the other way around.

"Let's get down to business," Jason stated as soon as the office doors closed.

D'Mari opened his briefcase and attempted to pull out a folder, but Jason stopped him.

"Cut the shit D'Mari Mitchell. I did all my research on you and your little cousins. The only reason I agreed to this meeting was to look good on paper, but there's nothing in that briefcase that can make me do business with *niggers* like you," Jason said with a voice full of disgust.

Everything came full circle to D'Mari in that very moment. On one hand, he couldn't believe his ears, but on the other, he knew that he was dealing with an *Uncle Tom* when he saw that there was a white *wanna be black* receptionist.

"I'm pretty sure I have something in this briefcase that can make you change your mind, but too bad I don't even give a fuck if you change it or not," D'Mari mused and pulled out his nine with the silencer and sent one bullet right between Jason's eyes.

"That's for *niggers* like me, muthafucka!" D'Mari spat and clicked on the camera button on the computer. He smiled when he noticed that the video wasn't even recording, but he wiped everything clean anyway, sent a text to The Rock Boyz, and dipped out of the side door.

3

"Well Mr. Washington, that concludes our tour of the property. Have you decided on which one of the three you'd like to buy?" Nicole, his realtor, asked with a smile.

Corey continued to look over the property, ignoring Nicole's lustful stares. Out of all the properties they viewed that day, the one they were standing in was the largest, which was what he was shopping for. The longer he stared around the room, his vision became clear of what they were going to use the property for.

"This is straight. I'll take it."

"Great. I'll write up the paperwork and have it to you by the end of the week. Is that okay with you?" She licked her lips seductively.

"Yeah. That's cool. Thank you for your time," Corey extended his hand.

Nicole quickly grabbed it and shook it while she eyed Corey from head to toe. Snatching his hand away, Corey turned to leave without saying another word. Unlocking the door to his Yukon Denali, Nicole called out after him, causing him to turn around.

"Mr. Washington, I usually don't do this, but I was wondering if I could take you out for dinner sometime this week," she asked with confidence.

Corey couldn't help but chuckle at her boldness.

"I'm gonna have to decline ya offer shawty," he continued to his car.

"Damn sexy," she grabbed his arm. "You just gonna turn me down without giving me a reason?"

"I got plans on fucking my wife tonight. I would bring you along, but she don't like to share." Corey snatched away from her and hopped in his truck, leaving her dumbfounded.

He laughed as he watched Nicole storm off. Starting his truck, Corey checked his cell phone. When he read the text from D'Mari saying the deal was cancelled, he knew what that meant. His meeting either ended on decent or deadly terms. Niggas needed to understand that shit was going to get done with or without their bitch asses. Corey shot a text to the chat before pulling out of the spot and heading towards the expressway, letting them know that he was about to check out the trap spots that J.R. told him about. Adamsville was the first stop on his list.

Taking the exit towards MLK Boulevard, Corey passed the famous Cascade skating rink before arriving at his destination ten minutes later. He parked his truck across the street from what he assumed was the trap spot and observed. There were a couple niggas posted up by a nearby store who were the local fiends. Every thirty minutes to an hour, one of the niggas headed down the block and dipped into the trap house. Then, he came out a few minutes and posted up in the same spot and repeated the same routine. After Corey watched them for a few hours, he checked out a few other spots in Adamsville before moving on the next area on his list.

By the time Corey was done casing the well-known trap spots, it was going on seven o'clock in the evening and he had more than enough info to report to his brothers about which spots they needed to run down on first. After handling business all day, he headed to the A for his weekly dice game. Pulling up to the spot, he saw that the place was packed, which meant it was money in the building and Corey was ready to take it.

Since him and his wife Alyssa moved to Georgia, shit immediately changed for him. He had a job as a sports commentator at a local sports network. Three weeks into his permanent and well-paying position, Corey stepped away from the legit life to go into business with his brothers, which was something he was getting used to. When it came to the streets, that nigga felt like a fish out of water. He was still learning the ins and out of the game; and although at times he felt like he should've stayed at his job, Corey wanted to be a part of the empire his family was building.

An hour later, Corey strolled out of the building a few hundred dollars richer, which put a smile on his face. Unlocking the doors to his truck, he heard his phone ringing in the passenger seat and quickly answered when he saw it was D'Mari.

"Wassup cuz?"

"That's what I need to be asking you," he sounded annoyed.

"What you mean?"

"Ya wife just called Drea looking for you. She said you were supposed to meet her at the Old Lady Gang for dinner by 8:45 and that she's been blowing ya phone up for the past two hours."

"Ahhh shit! I got caught up in casing the spots that I lost track of time. Fuck!" he disclosed.

"We'll talk about that shit another time. Just hurry ya ass and get to ya wife, C."

"Aight."

Ending the call, Corey brought the car to life and peeled out of the lot with screeching tires. Driving twenty miles over the speed limit, he made it to the restaurant fifteen minutes later, parking his truck in the nearest spot. Corey popped the trunk, grabbed his suit jacket, grabbed an emergency gift that he kept on standby, and closed the trunk. Corey strolled inside the restaurant and gave his name to the hostess who told him where his guest was sitting. He walked to the other side of the restaurant and locked eyes with a pissed off Alyssa.

"Hey bae," Corey bent down and kissed her cheek before sitting across from her.

Alyssa didn't respond. She continued to stare at him.

"Alyssa, I'm sorry that I'm late. I got caught up at work and lost track of time," he lied with a straight face. "Here. This is for you," he handed his wife the gift, but she didn't take it.

Alyssa remained quiet.

Corey let out a sigh of frustration as he ran his hand over his waves.

"Baby, I done already apologized. What else do you want me to say?"

"I want you to tell what the fuck is going on with you Corey," she spoke through gritted teeth, leaning forward.

"I don't know what you talking about Lyssa. I'm straight."

"Nigga don't give me that bullshit. I know something is going on with you because lately, you've been acting different and ya ass is *always* showing up late for shit."

"When was the last time I showed up late for something Alyssa?"

"How about two days ago when you were supposed to meet me at the mall for lunch to shop for the baby and ya ass *never* showed. I blew ya phone up and you *never* called me back. You didn't even shoot me a text letting me know what was going on, and when ya ass finally decided to bring ya ass home at damn near midnight, you gave me the same tired ass story about you being at work," she shouted in a whisper.

Even though she tried to keep the conversation between us, Corey knew that the people sitting on each side of them heard their conversation by the glances they received.

"Alyssa, can we just talk about this shit when we get home? You are attracting attention."

"I don't give a fuck if these motherfuckas are listening. I want answers got damnit and I want them *now*, Corey," she fussed.

"Look, I already told you what the deal is. I got tied up at work. If you don't want to believe that, then I don't know what to tell ya ass."

The couple stared at each other for a moment until the waiter appeared at the table with a bag in hand. Alyssa thanked him for the food before passing him a C note for his tip.

"What the fuck is this?" Corey pointed at the bag in her hand.

"Since you can't seem to be on time for me or keep it real, I'm taking my food to go. You can sit here and eat by ya damn self. I'll see you when you get home… that is *if* you decide to come home."

Alyssa got up from the table, purposely nudging him in his head as she passed. Corey remained at the table looking stupid and feeling like shit. Everything that Alyssa was saying was the truth, but he wasn't man enough to be honest with her. Yeah, she was his wife and they had no secrets; but he knew that if he revealed the truth, it would destroy their marriage. Corey didn't tell his wife that he quit his job or about the business he was building with his brothers. His carelessness was starting to get the best of him, and he knew he needed to get a handle on that shit before his behavior got any worse.

Leaving the restaurant ten minutes later, Corey arrived at his house in Douglasville thirty minutes later. He parked his car in the garage and made his way upstairs to his room only to find that the door was locked. Turning the door knob a couple more times, Corey pounded on the door.

"Alyssa open the fucking the door. This shit ain't funny!"

"Come on Alyssa! Look... I'm sorry for fucking up bae! I promise I'm gonna do better!"

He banged on the door a few more times before he decided to call it quits. Walking down the hall to the quest bedroom, Corey got undressed and climbed into bed. He stared up at the ceiling thinking of way to get a handle on his situation, and the only conclusion he had was to put on the charade he knew how.

4

D'Mani and J.R. strolled into what would be one of their new Atlanta traps and looked around at the way things were coming together. Although, they still needed to somewhat furnish it and get a crew together, D'Mani had high hopes that it wouldn't be too much longer before they had it up and running.

Since Atlanta was J.R.'s city, he had provided a few niggas who knew the area and were willing to put in work, coupled with some of D'Mani and D'Mari's New York people. They still had to make sure them niggas worked well together and that it wouldn't be no bullshit in any of the ten houses they would be running.

"So, when your guys supposed to be comin' down?" J.R. asked as they walked through the small, ranch style house, observing the team of Mexicans that were installing secret compartments into various areas of the floors, walls, and ceilings.

"In another week or so, the two houses over in Adamsville ain't really ready yet. Before we put them to work though, we gotta get them niggas in the same room," D'Mani noted.

"Definitely. I already narrowed down who'd be best in what areas. My niggas ready whenever we say the word." Although J.R. wasn't initially in the drug game, there wasn't a hustle he couldn't learn, and he had caught on rather quickly to how things were ran. All they needed to do next was get their crew right and set up shop.

"Hell yeah! I'm ready to see what this down south money lookin' like myself," D'Mani nodded, giving him a dap before one of the workers stole his attention.

"Aye Paco! That shit ain't right man! I don't want the damn door to be obvious nigga! Blend that shit in like he doin'!" he barked, pointing at another guy across the room, whose skills in carpentry were clearly better than Paco's. The small Mexican shook his head and hurriedly went to correct the small compartment he'd been working on. D'Mani shook his head at the mistake. Shit like that was the reason he always made sure to check shit out as it progressed. The last thing they needed was a setback because they were long overdue to push Tessa out and take over Atlanta.

"Where Raul at?" D'Mani questioned loudly to no one in particular. Raul was the one who told these niggas what to do and basically supervised them while they worked.

"He went to the back." Someone called out, prompting D'Mani to head in that direction. Him and J.R. entered the last bedroom of the house where there was a security room of sorts. It displayed about ten monitors with split screens showing different angles of each room and the front and back of the house.

"Nigga, stop watchin' porn back here and get up front with yo team!" D'Mani joked when he saw Raul. He had been working with the brothers for years as a tech guy and almost anything else they might need. Raul was the true definition of a jack of all trades. He turned around in the swivel chair he was sitting in and grinned before slapping hands with both D'Mani and J.R., who he'd recently been introduced to.

"I ain't gotta watch no fuckin' flicks bro! I get mad bitches with yo hatin' ass," he laughed.

"Them 1-800 numbers don't count," D'Mani told him matter-of-factly as he took a seat in one of the other chairs that were there.

"This nigga stay hatin'. Light skin niggas comin' back, thanks to that nigga Clarence, add a lil bit of Spanish to yo game, and some nice ass 360's and you on... you know bitches love a nigga with good hair," he boasted.

"Fuck is a Clarence?" J.R. frowned in confusion. D'Mani couldn't lie; he had never heard of his ass either. He would ask Stasia if she knew later though.

"Queen's baby daddy man," Raul explained but both men sat with blank expressions. "Fuck it!" He waved them off with a chuckle.

"Yeah fuck it cause I don't even know who the fuck either of them muthafuckas is!" J.R. admitted.

"Ima ask y'all niggas to get some social media in y'all lives."

"Hell nah!" both J.R. and D'Mani said quickly. Facebook and shit wasn't nothing but a way to jam niggas up. It was full of flossing ass niggas and bitches and they already knew that. Raul shrugged unaware of their reasons but not really caring either way.

"Well, I'm pretty much done settin' up the cameras and shit. I'll fix it to where all of y'all will have access to every camera in every house though by the time I'm done," Raul said, finally getting down to business.

"That's what's up man, just hit one of our lines when you do." J.R. glanced at his watch before standing and bumping fists with Raul. "We gotta head out and take care of that one thing."

D'Mani nodded aware of what he meant. J.R. had found somebody that supposedly knew who had been shooting at them at the club. Although the men all figured that the hit came from Tessa, it was still a given that they would handle whoever was *directly* responsible. Meaning, they wanted the niggas that pulled the triggers first and foremost.

Considering their background, D'Mani was used to the dangers of the game he and his brother were swept up in; things were different for them now though. They each had formed their own families, so any threat needed to be handled in a timely manner. "So, where this lead at?" D'Mani asked after they had pulled off.

"Bankhead. I know a few niggas out that way," J.R. replied, taking a pull of the blunt. "They said they heard some shit about what happened." D'Mani gave him the side-eye.

"And you trust them?" he wanted to know.

"Nigga yeah, I said I know them... besides they in the same profession as me, so they ain't got no reason to be on no set up shit." J.R. explained.

"Ayite, if they look like they bouta get on bullshit though, Ima shootin' first and askin' questions later."

"Shiiiit me too!" J.R. let it be known and the men shared a laugh.

After giving D'Mani directions, they arrived at a rundown looking house with about four niggas standing outside of its gate. J.R. instructed D'Mani to pull right out front. Shutting off his engine, D'Mani checked to make sure his gun was on his hip before following J.R. up the walkway through a chorus of *"what's ups."*

"Sup, Breeze in here?" J.R. asked, slapping hands with one of the guys.

"Yeah his ass up in there," dude told him. "Gone head, he waitin' on you."

J.R. gave him a head nod and led the way up the concrete steps and inside the house, where they found Breeze sitting on a broken down couch playing *Black Opps* while a half naked bitch danced on the table in front of him. When he saw them enter, his face split into a wide grin and he stood up to greet J.R. with a pound.

"Sup man, I ain't think you was comin'... yo ass took so long," Breeze chuckled and extended a hand out to D'Mani. "What's good?"

"Shit we just had some shit to take care of and it took longer than we thought," J.R. threw a look at D'Mani who shrugged, unbothered.

"It's cool, I wasn't doin' shit anyway," Breeze said, returning to his spot on the couch. "Have a seat y'all."

"Nah, we shouldn't be here too long," J.R. told him dryly as the girl on the table danced harder to try and gain his attention.

"Ayite. Aye Nette get yo hoe ass up outta here! These niggas don't want you in they face!" Breeze hissed at the girl, causing her to giggle stupidly. She still hopped her dumb ass down off the table and switched away, giving D'Mani and J.R. long stares.

"Man I swear to God that hoe be thirsty as hell." He grimaced, obviously embarrassed by her behavior; but both D'Mani and J.R. were used to the attention they gained from the opposite sex and had pretty much mastered ignoring it.

"Ayite so what you know man? I gotta get back to my girl," D'Mani finally said once she'd left the room. Breeze looked to J.R. for approval to speak on the situation before he finally said something.

"It ain't too much," he spoke slowly. "But a couple weeks ago, one of the niggas we been casin' was all up in the club talkin' shit about some out of town niggas that him and his crew was bustin' at for his boss." He looked between the two men like he'd just dropped a huge bomb on them.

"That's all you got?" D'Mani wanted to know. "You know how many out of town niggas he could have been talkin' bout?" he frowned and threw a look at J.R., who waved him off.

"It ain't many that came from New York and is settin' up shop around here," Breeze pointed out, quieting D'Mani. "Look, I figured it was worth looking into... so y'all want the nigga name or not?"

"Hell yeah!" J.R. answered for the both of them.

"Bet... the nigga name is Dex. He ain't shit but a lieu-tenant... but the nigga floss like he the big dog. He work for Tessa. If you tryna find his ass, it ain't gone be too hard... he be in Blue Flame tryna cash out every weekend," Breeze finished.

"Ayite man... good lookin'." J.R. leaned over and bumped fists with him before motioning for them to leave.

"Already my nigga." Breeze had his attention focused back on the t.v. before they had even hit the door.

Once they were in the car, D'Mani started it up and pulled off, but he couldn't help but to ask. "You think that shit accurate?"

"Shit Ion know, but it ain't gone hurt to check," J.R. said and D'Mani had to agree. He would rather have something than the nothing that they'd been working with.

"So, we hittin' up the club this weekend then?"

"Yeah and Ima ask Lexie if she ever heard of that nigga since she used to work there." D'Mani nodded, silently agreeing that asking Lexie about the nigga was smart.

Thirty minutes later, he had dropped J.R. off to his car and was finally making his way home to his make shift family when a call from his girl Stasia came through.

"What's up bae?"

"Hey, are you on your way home?" she questioned and he could hear her son Kyler running around and playing in the background.

"Yeah, you need somethin'?"

"Can you stop at the store and grab some butter and some eggs? I forgot to get some and I need it for the cornbread." She sounded like she was out of breathe and D'Mani knew it was because she was probably chasing Kyler around the house, and he couldn't help but chuckle. Although Kyler was Stasia's son from a previous relationship, D'Mani had accepted him as his own. They had gotten close over the course of him and Anastasia's relationship and he loved his little bad ass.

"I got you. I should be there in like a half hour." He informed her as he turned into the nearest store, which happened to be a Wal-Mart. D'Mani hated how packed the store always was, so he tried to limit his time going there; but he figured he could get in and out if he used self checkout.

"Okay thanks baby," she said.

"No problem." He disconnected the call as he parked in the fire lane and got out, making sure to hit the locks. D'Mani made it through the store quickly and made it to the dairy section, snatching up a tub of butter and one carton of eggs with eighteen in it. With his items in hand, he turned around and ran right into someone, damn near smashing the eggs into his clothes.

"Damn, watch where you goin'," D'Mani growled angrily.

"Oh, I'm sorry! I wasn't payin' atten...tion," her voice trailed off as they both realized that they knew each other.

"Cheyanne?"

"D'Mani?"

They both said at the same time, staring at each other in

awe. Cheyanne had been one of the longest relationships that D'Mani had. At one point in his life, he thought that he was going to marry her until him and D'Mari's lifestyle got in the way. Cheyanne was one of those good girls that wasn't into street shit or bad boys. D'Mani was honestly surprised that she had given him the time of day, but she had; and they had been good together. She was finishing up her last year of college when she told him that she was leaving to pursue a job opportunity in Chicago. Although he'd tried to get her to stay or at least let him come with her, she was adamant that they should part ways.

As bad as D'Mani wanted to be with her, he was young and didn't really feel the need to beg any female to be with him, so he let her go. He'd be lying if he said that he hadn't thought of her after that, but it was one of those things that you find a way to get over. Before he could say anything else, she chuckled uncomfortably.

"How have you been?" she asked, looking around.

"I been straight. I see things didn't work out in Chicago?" D'Mani hinted, hoping for a little bit of her time. He was happy with Anastasia, but he couldn't help feeling as if Cheyanne was the one that got away.

"Uhhhh... no, we moved here about two years ago," she sighed, and he could tell that it was something that she didn't really want to talk about.

"Oh, we-?"

"Mommy can I have this?" a little voice sounded from behind her and D'Mani met eyes with his twin in the form of a little girl. He looked at Cheyanne with narrowed eyes, but she avoided his gaze.

"Yes Imani," she forced out, trying to turn away. "It was nice seeing you." She told him, trying to leave except D'Mani grabbed her by the arm and stopped her from leaving.

"You already know what I'm askin' you... don't play with me Chey," he gritted and noticed that she was tearing up, but he didn't care. If his calculations and eyes were correct then.......

"Yes D'Mani, she's yours."

$$\text{🦂} \quad 5 \quad \text{🦂}$$

"Aye Alexis!" J.R. yelled from the top of the stair case in his Duluth home.

Ever since the shooting two weeks ago, he had been staying there, laying low, trying to stay off the radar. He loved the five-bedroom house, but it was too far from the city; and Atlanta traffic didn't make the commute any better. He thought more and more about selling his other condo and focusing on that property. Lexi also had a townhouse in the city that they were wasting money on because she was always at his crib with him. He figured that they'll sit down and talk about it eventually, especially since the couple was welcoming their first child in a few months.

"What's up Jeremy?" she finally replied from the kitchen.

J.R. took flight down the stairs and joined her as she sat at the kitchen table eating a bowl of ice cream.

"It's ten in the morning, why the fuck you eating that shit?" he asked while going into the stainless steel refrigerator and grabbing the milk.

"Because you inconsiderate and selfish," she spat.

J.R. closed the fridge door before turning around, staring

at her. Lexi was already a piece of work, but with the pregnancy and hormones, he never knew what was going to come out of her mouth.

"The fuck I do?" he quizzed.

"You nutted in me, that's what the fuck you did... and now I've been up all morning eating ice cream and flaming hots because that's the only thing I can keep doooowwww....."

Lexi ran off out of the kitchen through the living room and to the bathroom that was on the main level. J.R. listened as she emptied her ice cream and flaming hots into the toilet bowl. He laughed to himself as he dropped three ice cubes into the Frosted Flakes and milk he prepared. He then went to the counter, grabbed a banana, pilled and sliced it, and tossed it into his breakfast as well. Once he returned everything back to its rightful place, Lexi returned with the look of death on her face.

"Was you in here laughing at me?" she asked, grabbing more chips out of the cabinet.

"Nah baby but my lil mans in there fucking you up," he chuckled, walking to her, rubbing her slightly harden belly.

Lexi was almost four months and J.R. was excited to see that she was beginning to show.

"Lil man? You mean lil mama," she corrected him.

"I only make boys shorty," he stated.

"Aw... so you got some sons out here I don't know about?

"Shiiiidddd... maybe a few," he joked, but Lexi punched him in the chest anyway.

"But nah for real. I gotta ask you sum. You know a nigga name Dex?" he quizzed.

"Dex. Dex. Dex...." she repeated.

"Nah, I don't know him. Why what's up?"

"Shit, I just heard he was a regular at Blue Flame," he told her.

"Nope. Never heard of him," Lexi shrugged before grabbing her chips and heading out of the kitchen.

J.R. sat at the table and thought about the information that Breeze gave him and D'Mani. He said the nigga Dex wasn't a big deal, but J.R. knew he was trying to prove a point to Tessa by knocking him off. He wasn't able to get more info about the dude, but J.R. was the type of nigga who rather go to the source directly and that's what he planned on doing.

Once he was done eating, he headed upstairs, showered, and prepared to get his day started.

J.R. stopped at the gas station to fill his tank before hitting 285. He planned on spending as little time in the city as possible. Lexi had been bugging lately about him always being in the streets, so he figured he'll surprise her later with a date night; but first, he needed to take care of something. J.R. turned down the radio once he made it to his exit. After bussing a few rights and a left, he pulled in front of D'Mani and Stasia's crib and blew the horn. J.R. waited for what seemed like thirty minutes to an impatient nigga like him before grabbing his phone and calling D'Mani. The phone rang and rang before going to the voicemail.

"This nigga," he mumbled as he opened the door to get out.

Before his Air Force Ones could hit the concrete, Mani came hopping down the stairs.

"Nigga, you knew I was on my way," J.R. snapped before his brother-in-law could get comfortable in the leather seats of his truck.

"Yeah mannnn... my bad, I dozed off on the couch," Mani replied, never looking J.R.'s way.

"You good?" he glanced over at Mani and then back at the road.

He could tell by the tone in his voice that something was bothering him.

"Mannnn bro, shit crazy," he sighed.

J.R. didn't want to pry, especially if Mani didn't want to elaborate any further. The two of them was cool, but they mainly kept everything business. Just as J.R. was about to reply, his phone rang; he looked down at it on his lap before answering.

"Yeah girl, I'm on my way. As a matter of fact, you can come out," he said into the phone before hanging up.

"Who dat... Lexi?" Mani quizzed as he placed the weed inside the blunt.

"Nah this other shorty," J.R. replied nonchalantly.

"Other shorty? J.R., Lexi gon' kick yo...... DAMN SHE BAD!"

J.R. laughed as they watched Katrina walk to the car. She was wearing a pair of white shorts and a white crop top with the word *"PETTY"* written in red. He couldn't stunt, Trina was bad, but she was dumb as a box of rocks and that alone was a turnoff.

"What's up baby? Heyyyyy baby friend!" Trina spoke and flirted with D'Mani at the same time.

"Gone shorty. I got too many problems already," Mani said, dismissing her with his hands while staring out the window.

J.R. laughed out loud. It felt good to know that Lexi wasn't the only Holiday sister who was crazy.

"What you got for me?" he asked, focusing his attention back on her and the reason he was there.

Katrina licked her lips seductively and leaned closer towards the window. J.R. felt his dick rising in his jeans but homie downstairs was just gon' have to be disappointed. Wasn't no way in the world he would ever fuck with Trina again.

Trina went inside the fake Gucci purse she was wearing and pulled out a yellow manila folder. She handed the package to J.R. who thanked her for her services before pulling off.

"You still hitting that?" Mani asked, choking on the smoke from the weed.

"Hell nah!" he answered quickly.

"Good because bitches like her ain't shit but trouble," he spoke.

"Nigga is you good?" J.R. looked over and asked.

It was obvious that something was on Mani's mind and whatever it was, it was fucking with him.

"Look right, after I left you the other day, I stopped at Wal-Mart and ran into my first love who I haven't seen in a while. I didn't even know she was living in Atlanta, but long story short, she had her daughter with her and....."

"I don't wanna know.... NOPE! Don't tell me *shit* cuz when shit hit the fan, Lexi gon' ask if I knew and why I ain't tell her and mannnnnn...... I ain't trying to be into it with that girl," J.R. spoke.

D'Mani laughed out loud, but J.R. was dead ass serious; he knew how that shit worked far too well.

"Yeah nigga, that's my daughter and..... "

"So just fuck what I said huh?" J.R. hissed.

"Nigga, I had to tell somebody," D'Mani chuckled.

J.R. shook his head and listened while D'Mani told his story. He had no advice for him because truthfully, he wouldn't know what to do if he was in the same bind. He was just happy that it wasn't him. After driving another thirty minutes and smoking two more blunts, the duo made it to their destination high as giraffe's pussy.

J.R. put the blunt out before checking his surroundings.

"Where we at?" Mani asked as he scanned things as well.

"Aw, I didn't tell you?" J.R. replied, reaching in the back seat, fumbling through a bag.

"Nah, you ain't tell me shit."

"You strapped?" J.R. asked.

"Always but...."

"Cool. Throw this on and let's go."

J.R. tossed D'Mani a black ski mask. D'Mani examined it with a look of confusion plastered on his face.

"Nigga, we finna rob some shit? Why the fuck you ain't tell me? I ain't prepared," Mani grimaced.

"If you strapped, then you always prepared. This one of Tessa's trap houses. He a lieutenant that ain't *shit* without his soldiers. We kill them and the rest will fall in line," J.R. said, cocking his pistol and getting out of the car.

6

"I can't find nothing to wear," Drea whined.

"Andrea, you have more clothes than a department store. Why you trippin' bae?"

"Trippin'? Why I gotta be trippin' because I said I can't find nothing to wear... you know what? I don't even wanna go," she snapped.

D'Mari was frustrated as fuck, but he was trying his best not to let it show. Drea had been moody as fuck lately, and every time he asked her about it, she told him that she was fine. Out of all the damn clothes she had in the closet, she should have been able to walk in and out in a matter of seconds. On top of that, he had some shit on his mind that needed to be addressed with the boyz; but he was hoping that it was all just a small misunderstanding and that he had overlooked some shit.

"Maannn... Drea calm down and just find something to throw on. Better yet, I'll find you something," he suggested and walked into the closet.

He heard Drea smack her lips and automatically knew that an eye roll followed, but he proceeded forward and grabbed a black and gold dress that she had recently bought while on one of her mall trips with her sisters. It seemed as if the confident woman that had he had once known was slowing withering away. He knew that their relationship had moved really fast, considering the circumstances, but he loved her ass; she was just not the same since she had given birth to the twins. If someone would have told D'Mari that he would end up marrying someone that he had a one night stand with, he would call them a muthafuckin' lie. Nonetheless, he loved Drea and hoped that whatever was going on with her wasn't anything that would last too long.

"We don't have to go. I'll just stay home."

D'Mari rubbed his closed eyes and rubbed his temples. He felt a headache coming on. A shot of Jack Daniels was calling his name. It was definitely a brown kinda day.

"Drea... baby what's wrong?

"Nothing is wrong D'Mari. I just can't find shit to wear. I don't even wanna go for real. Just leave," she fussed.

"One minute you fine, then the next you spazzin' out. Like what the fuck is the problem? I can't fix it if I don't know."

"Ain't shit for you to fix... just leave. You probably wanna go out wit someone else anyway."

"You know what... Ima just leave like you said because I'm not bout to argue over nothing," D'Mari grabbed his phone and left out.

He heard Drea talking shit, but he really wasn't the arguing type, so he ignored her. He knew that she would be on the phone with her sister shortly talking shit, but Mari knew he hadn't did shit wrong. After making a pit stop to kiss the twins goodbye and talking to his in-laws, he made his way outside and hopped in his car. As soon as he pulled out of the driveway, Mari placed a phone call to Corey.

"What's up cuz?" Corey answered after the third ring.

"Maannn what you on?" Mari quizzed.

"Shit... just out and about handling some business. What's goin' on?"

"Drea buggin' and I need to holla at you about some shit anyway. Meet me at the bar them girls was talkin' about that day... wasn't it Tracey's Bar & Grill or some shit like that?

"Yeah that's it. Lyssa love the wings from there so that's perfect. I can grab her some food and she'll be aight when I make it in."

"Bet," Mari responded and ended the call.

D'Mari cruised down 285 with the traffic while listening to some HOV. Ever since the night of their official meeting, at least once a week Mari found himself rapping along with Jay to their theme song. The shit always hyped him up. Twenty minutes later, he arrived at his destination and parked. Not knowing exactly how far away Corey was, D'Mari decided to go on inside and cop a table or booth, or whatever they had to offer. Once inside, he seated almost immediately and Mari ordered a double shot of Jack on the rocks without even waiting on his cousin. When the waitress brought his drink back, Mari downed half of it and then Corey arrived at the table.

"Damn... you didn't even wait on my ass."

"Listen... I don't know what's wrong wit Drea ass, but she been trippin' big time. Her moods change so fuckin' fast, I don't be knowing what the hell to say," Mari vented.

"Bruh... she probably goin' through that shit... what you call it? You know after women have babies? I don't know what it is but Google it."

"It's called postpartum. What can I get for you?" the waitress reappeared and interrupted.

"Yeah... that shit. Thanks ma, and let me get a double shot of Patron and some wings. A double order for here and an order to go."

"And I'll take another the drink... same way," Mari requested.

"Ima have to do some research on that shit... we gotta get back to normal," Mari said and finished off his drink.

"Yeah... you know Drea is the level headed one, so she ain't spazzin' for no reason."

"You right, but I need to run some other shit by you right..." D'Mari started saying, but Corey's phone rang and interrupted the conversation.

D'Mari didn't know what had been said on the other end, but it left Corey looking crazy.

"You aight?" he asked his cousin after he hung up.

"Yeah man... Lyssa just been buggin' a little bit but what's up?"

"Oh yeah... I know you the money genius and shit, but did you happen to see that the numbers was off the last few times?"

There was an awkward moment of silence before Corey replied.

"Man cuz... I was hoping I was wrong, but I see you caught it too. We short on that nigga Boosie end. I been watching him and I was actually gon' holla at him tomorrow anyway. I can't believe it," Corey confessed.

"Boosie? That nigga been wit us for years. You put him on. You mean to tell me he moved down here wit us to start stealing?" D'Mari quizzed.

"That's exactly how I was feeling. I didn't wanna believe it, but numbers don't lie."

"Damn shol' don't... that needs to be handled ASA-mutha-fuckin'-P," Mari expressed and he noticed the somber look on Corey's face.

It was his boy from the jump, so it would only be right if he handled it.

"You gon' be able to take care of it or do ..."

TWYLA T.

"I got it cuz... I got it."

7

Corey sat next to D'Mari with his mind racing as he thought about what he'd just done. The discussion about the vanishing money was playing heavily in his mind. He thought that the drinks would help ease his anxiety but that shit just made him slip into a state of depression and fear. Corey was trying his best to keep his composure, but he felt like he was slowly but surely spinning out of control. The phone called he received only added to his stress and the fact that he couldn't confide in anyone about it, not even his wife, had him living an unstable life.

After a few buffalo wings, Corey pushed his plate away and downed the rest of his drink. Placing his head in his hands, the guilt from the lie he'd just told his cousin was beginning to get the best of him. Corey was ready to confess about the sins he'd committed, but after taking a few moments to consider the consequences of his confession, he decided against it.

"Yo cuz. You aight?" D'Mari asked with food in his mouth.

"A nigga just been stressed the fuck out lately cuz." He removed his hands from his face. "I've been trying to keep shit under wraps with Alyssa, but it seems like I keep fucking up one way or another. I'm so caught up with business that I'm missing out on important shit with my wife," he halfway confessed.

"Besides being late for dinner, what else have you been late for?" D'Mari pushed his food to the side.

"Shit, what *haven't* I been late for? Lunch date, dinner dates, and shopping excursions for the baby," Corey shook his head. "Alyssa is used to me being there for her whenever she needs me. I don't know how to balance this shit out." He flagged down the bartender and ordered another drink.

"Look, I know this street shit ain't easy, and I appreciate the hours you've been clocking and helping us get shit in motion; but you *always* gotta make sure home is taken care of. Ya wife is pregnant and holding down a job. You basically gave up ya old life and jumped head first into a new one." The waitress placed their drinks of front of them and walked away. "How about this, whenever you gotta meet wifey for something and you're handling business, let one us know and we'll handle business until you return," his cousin suggested.

"Shit, that sounds like a plan," they shook hands.

"We know you a rookie to this shit," D'Mari chuckled. "We can't have Alyssa being suspicious and shit. You know how her and her sisters are," he gave Corey a knowing look.

Corey nodded his head in agreement.

Tossing their drinks back, they chopped it up for a few more minutes before paying their tab, grabbing the food, and leaving out. Promising that he was going to handle that situation with Boosie, Corey jumped in his truck and started his car. When his cousin was gone, he went into the glove compartment and removed one of the many pill bottles he had stashed there. Examining the pill bottle, Corey debated on whether or not he should pop the *perks* that have been helping him deal with the stress of his new lifestyle.

Throwing caution to the wind, he popped two pills then drove out of the parking lot.

Barely making it home, Corey pulled into his driveway, killing the engine. Feeling the effects of the drugs and alcohol, he rested his head on the window, taking a moment to get himself together. Thinking of his upcoming mission, Corey was fucked up about what he had to do to his homie Boosie, but what fucked him up the most was what he did to him. He tried to convince himself that he was doing the right thing but deep down, he really felt bad for his boy. Allowing his '*I don't give a fuck*' attitude to kick in, Corey shrugged it off and charged it to the game.

Stumbling in the house, he closed the door behind him and found his wife chilling on the couch in the living room. Dipping into the kitchen, he quickly splashed water on his face, dried his face off with his shirt, and joined her.

"Well, well, well. Look who made it home before midnight," a sarcastic Alyssa spoke dryly as she rubbed her belly.

"I guess I deserve that and I know this won't solve our problems, but I got wings from ya favorite spot," Corey handed her the bag.

Staring between him and the bag, Alyssa snatched the bag from his hand, causing him to laugh as he sat down beside her.

"You're right. This doesn't change shit. It's like you went from being over protective of me to not giving a fuck about me at all, Corey."

"Are you serious?"

Alyssa shot him a look that let him know to stop playing with her.

"Aight." He held his hands up. "Look bae, I done tried to make you shit right with you since you left my ass at the restaurant. Tell me what to do so I can make shit right

39

between us. I'm tired of sleeping in that damn guest room, Lyssa."

"Okay. How about being here more and stop forgetting about me. I know that you're working hard and everything, but you still need to make time for me. If you keep coming in late and you stop being there for me now, what the hell is gonna happen when the baby comes? I don't wanna be raising the baby by myself, Corey," she gazed at him with teary eyes.

Corey's heart broke seeing how hurt his wife was behind his actions. Wrapping his arms around his wife, he embraced her tightly.

"I'm sorry I haven't there for you when you needed, but I give you my word that I'm gonna do better. I promise. Aight?"

"Okay," Alyssa sniffled.

"Does that mean I can sleep with you tonight?" He kissed her cheek then her neck.

"Mmm hmm but first you gotta brush ya teeth because that Patron on ya breath is about to make me puke," she pushed him away.

"Damn. You just gonna play me like that?"

"Yup. Go handle that."

Corey kissed her cheek once more before heading up to his room, heading straight to the bathroom. Placing the toothpaste on the brush, his phone began to ring, and when he saw it was D'Mani calling, he knew what the deal was.

"Wassup D'Mani?"

"Mari just told me about Boosie. Are you sure about that shit?"

"You think I would lie on my nigga for no reason, man?" he retorted.

The phone fell silent.

"My bad. D'Mari told me that you were gonna handle it but don't worry about it. I got it, aight."

"Aight."

"I'll holla at you later."

Ending the call, Corey stared at himself in the mirror. Finding comfort in the lie he recited again, he brushed his teeth and prayed that God wouldn't kill him in his sleep.

🏶 8 🏶

"What the fuck you just say! I can't hear you my nigga!" D'Mani taunted as he looked down at a wide eyed Boosie, who sat tied to a chair in the center of the basement.

"Mmmmhhpphmmm!" The room was filled with the sounds of his muffled cries, but it didn't seem to bother D'Mani or anyone else in the room. Even if it had though, nobody dared say anything knowing that they would meet the same fate.

"Shut yo bitch ass up!" D'Mani barked and sent a teeth chattering right hook to dude's face, prompting him to be silent.

"I want y'all to pay attention cause this the only warnin' I'm offerin' up! Don't play with our fuckin' money! Bet not be no flossin' in the club, no trickin' on bitches, and for damn sure not no stealin'! Cause I'm gone find out and you gone get done just how this nigga bout to!" He preached, making sure to lock eyes with every one of the workers in attendance before turning his attention back to Boosie. The nigga continued making noise and struggling against the ropes that bound him. Although it wouldn't make a difference what he had to say, his ass was dying no matter what lie fell from his lips, but D'Mani couldn't help but to be curious.

"Fuck you tryna say so damn bad?" he questioned with his head cocked to the side as he snatched the duck tape from off Boosie's mouth.

"D, man listen." He started and then paused sucking in a deep breath. "I swear on my mama I ain't take that shit! I wouldn't do no shit like that bro."

"So you callin' my brother and my cousin some fuckin' liars nigga!?" D'Mani prepared to hit him again.

"Nooo!" he flinched. "It gotta be a misunderstanding man! I swear, just give me a chance to figure this shit out!"

D'Mani seemed to consider the offer briefly. On one hand Boosie *had* been a good worker up until the point that their money came up missing, but on the other hand, he didn't want to give the impression that niggas could get away with such an offense. With that thought in mind, his decision was made. Mani quickly retrieved his gun from his back, pointing it at Boosie's head.

"Rock Boys don't give out chances," he spat before sending a single bullet into the center of his head. The room became deathly silent once the man was no longer pleading and D'Mani used the moment to address the remaining niggas that were there.

"This type of shit is avoidable, don't be like Boosie, and let greed be the reason your life get cut short," were his last words to the men before he dismissed them and shot a quick text to the cleanup crew.

"Nigga, that shit just took way too long." J.R. finally spoke once they were alone. He'd been sitting quietly occupied with his phone while D'Mani handled Boosie. It was clear he had something on his mind, but J.R. wasn't the type to talk too much; so if he did have anything going on, D'Mani doubted he'd talk to him about it.

"I barely did shit."

J.R. raised a brow and looked around D'Mani to where Boosie's body sat, full of blood from the beat down he'd received. D'Mani had spent half an hour alone kicking his ass before removing three of the fingers on the man's right hand. D'Mani followed his gaze and let out a sigh.

"Ayite, maybe I went a lil too hard."

"Ya think nigga." J.R. said sarcastically, getting up from the chair he had been sitting in and moving to leave the basement with D'Mani right behind him. The two men headed up the stairs, passing the cleanup crew on their way out of the house.

"Aye let me run somethin' by you right quick." D'Mani mused once they were seated inside of J.R.'s car and pulling away. He could see J.R. give him a look even in the dark car, but he had already told him about his situation and figured he might as well continue confiding in him.

"Here you go... this bet not be about that baby shit... I done told yo ass.."

"Listen nigga... it's eating me up and I gotta tell Stasia," Mani confessed.

"It was nice knowing you my nigga," J.R. laughed.

"Maannn this shit is old. She can't trip too hard."

"Nigga, if you really believed that, you wouldn't be trippin'."

D'MANI RODE IN SILENCE THE REST OF THE WAY. DEEP down, he felt like Stasia would understand. He hoped that he was right because before he knew it, he was pulling up at home.

"Ayite man, Ima get up with you tomorrow," J.R. finally spoke as they pulled up outside of D'Mani and Anastasia's house. D'Mani looked up at the four bedroom mini mansion that he had purchased for them and shook his head. Damn near all the lights were on, meaning that either Kyler was up playing or she was up waiting on his ass.

"Bet... we still gotta go see about that nigga Rex." D'Mani slowly got out of the car and made his way up to the door, where Anastasia stood waiting for him.

"Why the fuck you ain't been answerin' yo phone D'Mani?!" she hollered not even giving him a chance to get inside before she started going in. He stopped and admired her beautiful golden brown features before he decided to answer.

"You know I don't answer the phone when I'm takin' care of shit, Stasia don't play! Was it an emergency?" he asked, lowering his voice and stepping closer to her.

"No, but you always text or call to let me know you're okay," she whined, garnering a smile out of D'Mani.

"Ohhh so you missed daddy huh?"

Her attitude seemed to have simmered down momentarily and she let him pull her into an embrace before pulling back slightly and slapping his chest with her small fist. "Yes I miss you nigga. You been runnin' the streets so much I barely get to see you."

D'Mani instantly felt bad knowing that there was more to his absence than them expanding their business. True, he had been busy before, but ever since finding out about Imani, he could barely look his girl in the face knowing that he was keeping it from her. He let out a sigh and then ran a hand down his waves, looking down at her with hesitant eyes.

"You right ma, I know a nigga been a lil distant lately. I-I need to tell you somethin'." He felt Stasia's body get stiff in his arms and knew she was preparing herself to act a damn fool if need be. "Don't be like that." D'Mani pleaded, taking her by the hand and leading her over to the couch in the living room.

"What is it D'Mani? Don't stall, and you bet not come out yo face and say you cheatin' on me either! I'll kill you and that bitch!" she threatened even though they both knew she was lying. Anastasia had too much to lose to throw her life away over some small shit like that.

"Ain't no-damn-body cheatin'... I'm tryna tell you that I ran into an old girlfriend the other day."

"And?" she huffed.

"Let me finish," D'Mani said, sucking his teeth. She was making the confession harder than it needed to be, and he knew that if he didn't just spit it out, she would ultimately make him chicken out. "As I was sayin', I ran into an old girl-friend and......she let me know that we got a daughter together."

"Ahhhhh hell naw! You got me fucked up!" she hopped up out of her seat and started trying to swing on him. D'Mani blocked her hits and stood up himself, finally getting a grip on her hands.

"Calm yo ass down Ma! This shit old as hell, the baby fuckin' three years old!"

She seemed shocked by that little piece of information, and D'Mani could practically see the wheels spinning in her head before her face contorted into a nasty frown, and she stopped struggling against him.

"Get yo fuckin' hands off me!" she growled and he hesi-tated, unsure of whether or not he should do that. "I swear I won't hit you."

Slowly, D'Mani released the hold he had on her arms. Her chest rose and fell heavily as she stood there staring at him in silence. Trying to get a handle on her , he stepped closer.

"I guess I can't really be mad about something that

happened before me, but I'm damn sure gone need a minute to wrap my mind around this shit."

"I'm still in shock too bae, just don't shut down on me. We can get through this shit together." He started making an attempt to pull her in for a hug, but she held up a hand to stop him.

"I said I gotta wrap my mind around it, and you can sleep yo ass in another room while I do," she spat, cutting him off and walking away.

D'Mani released a breath he didn't realize he was holding before dropping down into the chair he'd been sitting in. He hadn't known what to expect when he told her, but he wasn't trying to be put out his damn bed over it. He couldn't help but hope that she figured out her feelings fast because he was already regretting even telling her.

9

"So J.R., you knew this whooollleee time that that fool D'Mani was hiding a baby from my sister and you ain't tell me?" Lexi snapped, pointing her long red nails in his face while one hand rested on her small hip.

J.R. rolled his eyes and let out a long sigh. He told D'Mani punk ass that he didn't want to know about that baby for this very reason.

"No baby, I didn't know," he huffed.

"That's funny because when Stasia asked D'Mani who all had he told, he named you. He said yo dirty ass name and no one ... SOOOOOO I pose this question to you AGAIN..."

"Man shut the fuck up. The nigga told me, but like you should be doing right now, I minded my own business. That man and the shit he got going on at home ain't got shit to do with *us*. You more worried about *her* nigga cheating than you are *your own*," J.R. barked, causing Lexi to take a few steps back.

"Why the fuck should I be worried about my man cheating in the first place?" she hissed, now stepping closer to him.

J.R. stood there silently trying to figure how D'Mani problem turned into his. Had he just kept his mouth closed or left out that last part, his girl wouldn't be standing her five-foot-five ass in front of him ready to fight.

"Look beautiful, you focused on the wrong shit. I'm about to go take care of some business and when I get home we....."

"WE ain't gon' do shit. You gon' get high and fall asleep. Bye Jeremy," Lexi dismissed him, turning and walking out the bedroom door.

J.R. shook his head and let her go. He ain't have time to be arguing with Lexi about the same shit that they've been arguing about for the past weeks. She was bitching every chance she got about him not spending time with her. J.R. could admit that since getting with the guys, he was home less, but it would pay off later and Lexi would understand.

After throwing on his shoes, J.R. grabbed his keys and a black plastic bag from the closet and went downstairs. When he made it down the stair landing, he found Lexi curled up on the couch on the phone. He would bet his last dollar that she was on three-way with her sisters, talking shit about him. Walking over to her, he kissed her on the forehead and dipped out.

J.R. drove 285 heading towards Bankhead to meet up with the guys. He arranged for all of them to meet him there, but they had no clue as to why. Getting in his zone, he grabbed the aux cord, put on Young Jeezy's album *"Thug Motivation,"* and did the dash. Arriving about forty-five minutes later, he pulled into the parking lot. He noticed that all the guys car was there and smiled. He hated waiting on people and what they were about to do next, there was no time to waste.

"Fuck!" he cursed to himself before turning back around and going back to the car.

J.R. opened the passenger's seat door and grabbed the

black plastic bag he left on the seat before hitting the alarm and continuing forward.

"How the fuck you gon' call a meeting and not be on time?" D'Mani yelled, his voice echoing in the empty warehouse.

"How the fuck you gon' snitch on me to my bitch sister?" J.R. yelled back.

"Damn man. My bad... I thought I texted you and warned you, but I told Stasia you knew about the baby," he replied.

"What baby?" Corey questioned.

"Who baby?" D'Mari quizzed.

"Man, fuck all that. Y'all can catch up later. Let's talk about why we are here," J.R. stated before he continued.

"Me and D'Mani went to holler at this shorty a few days ago. Shorty was able to get some information on that nigga Dex who is under Tessa's cartel. I thought getting close to him was going to be hard, but I was wrong. Shorty dropped some jewels and I can *guarantee* that either Dex is going to be dead or so pissed off that we gon' start a war for real. I need to know if you niggas down to ride?" he questioned.

"Without a doubt, let's move," D'Mani spoke up first, not even asking any questions.

"Shid, y'all riding, I'm riding." D'Mari seconded.

The three men looked at Corey who pulled his gun from his waist, which was all the confirmation they needed.

J.R. led everyone out of the back door to a white caravan. Pulling the keys from his pocket, everyone watched on and wondered what he had going on now.

"Look, it ain't no Maserati but it's gon' get shit done. Corey, you drive."

J.R. tossed him the keys and everyone piled in. Once settled, J.R. gave Corey directions before flaming up a blunt.

"You care to tell us what the fuck you got going on?" D'Mari asked, grabbing the blunt .

"Remember how them niggas shot at us at the club?" he asked to no one in particular and not waiting for an answer.

"Well, paybacks a motherfucker," he continued, rambling through the plastic bag he brought along with him.

"So where exactly are we headed?" Corey glanced out of the mirror and asked.

J.R. took the contents out of the bag and handed a shirt to each one of the guys and waited for their reaction.

"Where the fuck we going with these green ass shirts on?" D'Mani questioned.

"And who the fuck is the Smithe family and why we got their family reunion shit?" D'Mari chimed in.

"The way I look at it is, you want a motherfucker to feel pain, you bring it to their front door. No one is exempt," J.R. replied.

"Nigga is you serious? We about to shoot up a family reunion?" D'Mari quizzed.

"Nigga is you scared?" J.R. shot back.

"Look, all I'm saying is, I ain't trying to kill no kids," he stated.

"Me either, that's why y'all gotta work on ya aim. Ain't no more time to talk about the shit, make sure y'all loaded and let's go," he ordered as Corey pulled the white van into the park.

J.R. slid the doors of the van opened and smiled. He wasn't big on religion, but God had to be on his side at that very moment. When he opened the door, he literally ran into Dex, who was getting out of his car with his wife. Dex looked like he had seen a ghost as he tried to reach for his gun, but it was already too late. In broad daylight, J.R. emptied his clip inside of him, saving two bullets for his wife. Loud screams echoed the park, but J.R. was back in the van before their bodies hit the pavement. He was back in his seat before the other guys even made it out of the van.

"Guess we ain't gotta worry about popping no kids," Corey stated as he peeled off in traffic.

J.R. looked down at his ringing phone and declined the call from his little sister Yasmine. His main focus at that moment was ditching that van and getting away.

"So that nigga dead, what that mean for us?" Mari questioned.

"We took out Tessa's top hitter. We basically sending a message to that nigga that he's next. So shit about to get real. After we eliminate his cartel, we'll be in control over everything," J.R. explained, this time answering his phone as Yasmine called back for the sixth time.

"Aye sis, I'm handling some business right now, I'll hit you back," he quickly stated.

"NO JEREMY NO! IT'S MOMMA. SHE'S GONE J.R., SHE'S GONE!"

J.R. listened as his seventeen-year-old sister screamed into the phone. He had heard her loud and clear but refused to accept what she was saying.

"Look Yas, I'm on the first flight to Philly. I love you," was all J.R. said before staring out the window.

10

"Hey daddy's little princess," D'Mari picked Ava up and kissed her cheeks.

"Hey daddy's man," he gave DJ the same treatment after he put Ava back down.

The twins had just turned five months old the day before and were growing like crazy. It amazed D'Mari to see their growth every day. On May 5th, the day they were born, both of them were so tiny and Mari was scared shitless to even hold them. With Drea's coaxing, he got through it and it was one of the best days of his life.

"It's crazy how fast they're growing huh," Drea appeared right beside him smiling.

"They are... I'm glad they ain't no lil crybabies too."

"I know that's right. I would go crazy," Drea admitted.

Drea had been a good mood for the past couple of days, so Mari decided not to even mention the postpartum shit. He didn't want to bring up anything negative while things were going smooth. Mari looked at his wife and his dick began to get hard. After such an eventful day, he needed to relieve some stress and what better way was there to do it?

"Why you lookin' at me like that?" Drea quizzed.

"*He* want you," he replied and grabbed his dick.

"Boy you so damn stupid," she laughed.

"I'm so damn serious too," he grabbed her and pulled her towards the bedroom.

"The kids Mari," Drea whined.

"My mama will hear them if they cry. You just come on and give me some of this pussy."

D'Mari's mom had arrived the night before and he was trying to get to the room before her loud ass mouth came and fucked up his flow. One of the reasons that he never complained about Drea's Aunt Shirley was because his mom was damn near just like her. Whatever came to her mind came out of her mouth. Mari was glad that Drea's folks had left the other day because he wasn't sure if he could handle both women under one roof.

As soon as they made it to the room, he pushed Drea onto the bed and pushed her skirt all the way up. After he pulled her black laced pantie off, Mari dove head first into her pussy. Drea began to moan instantly and her sex cries turned Mari on and made him continue to pleasure her.

"Let that shit go baby, I want it in my mouth," he coaxed her.

Just like magic, Drea's legs began to shake and she cried out as she came. D'Mari welcomed her juices, and when her orgasm ended, he stood up and slipped out of his jeans and boxers. Drea tried to sit up, but he eased into her wetness and they both moaned.

"I... I was... tryna... return the favor," she said between strokes.

"I needed to feel this pussy. You can return the favor later."

D'Mari stroked Drea like he hadn't had any in months, but in reality, it had only been a about a week. The couple

54

didn't really talk much after their failed attempt at date night and Drea had been moody. The past few days, she had been better, but Mari still didn't take any chances. When she walked into the babies room looking all good and bubbly, he knew it was on then.

"Shit baby... you feel so good," Drea simpered.

He began hitting her spot, making her scream out in pleasure and pain.

"Y'all two left the babies to fuck... y'all ain't *shit*!" Ms. Mitchell could be heard saying from the hallway.

"Oh my God... get up," Drea tried to push Mari, but he wouldn't budge.

"She'll be aight," he leaned down and kissed Drea but never stopped beating her pussy up.

"Ahhh... You... make me... sick!" Drea dug into his back.

"Got damn," Mari grunted as he barely pulled out and shot cum all over Drea's legs.

He fell down beside her and a few minutes later, they both started laughing.

"You really ain't shit. You gon' have your mama talking shit about me."

"I told she'll be alright. You cooking tonight or you want me to grab something after my meeting?"

"Hmmm... I can cook. Who you meeting wit today?" Drea questioned as she sat up.

"I gotta link up wit the boyz about some business... shouldn't take more than an hour or so," Mari followed suit and got up.

"Y'all done got mighty close. What y'all got going on?"

"The less you know the better baby," he kissed her and went and washed up.

D'Mari could feel Drea staring at him, but she didn't say anything else. That was surprising as hell because Drea was nosey as fuck; and mixed with her being a lawyer, it was never easy to get shit by her for a long period of time. Mari meant what he said though, the less she knew the better.

Later that night, D'Mari pulled up to the meeting location, parked, and headed inside. Things were looking up for the Rock Boyz and he was happy about that. The incident revolving around Boosie still fucked with him a little. Boosie was actually Corey's boy, but they all had created a bond. Mari couldn't figure out why he would steal from them knowing that he could have any damn thing that he asked for. That was really water under the bridge, so he shrugged it off and made his way inside. When he walked in, Corey was sitting at the table talking on the phone and it appeared that he was arguing. D'Mari was shocked because he didn't see Corey's truck outside. As soon as they locked eyes, Corey ended the call.

"What's up cuz?" he greeted.

"Shit... I been having to get on these lil niggaz a lot lately. It's all good though."

"Where yo truck?"

"I been here for a minute going over numbers, so I just parked in the back."

"Oh... aight then," Mari replied and took a seat beside his cousin.

They chopped it up for a few minutes before D'Mani walked in. J.R. normally beat both Corey and D'Mani there, but he was nowhere in sight. Traffic was always a bitch, so D'Mari went and grabbed a Corona from the fridge to pass time.

"Bring me one too... me too nigga," his cousin and brother said.

The spot they were in was a building that they had purchased recently. It was low key and could be used for pretty much anything. Mari had a few ideas in mind, but the most important was to never be caught at the same spot too much just in case niggaz were following them. It was manda-tory to switch shit up. J.R. walked in just when D'Mari was about to call the meeting to order.

"My bad y'all... that call from earlier fucked me up," J.R. said and walked straight toward the kitchen.

Instead of grabbing a beer like the others, he walked back in the room with a bottle of Jack Daniels. He took two big swigs and then sat the bottle down on the table as he copped his seat.

"What happened man?" Mani inquired before anyone else could.

"My OG had a brain aneurism and didn't make it. I'm catching a flight to Philly in a few hours," J.R. sighed.

"Aww damn man. Sorry to hear that."

"Fuck man... we here for ya... yeah man we got you."

All of the boyz gave their condolences and sat in silence. J.R. broke the silence and started reminiscing about his mom and his life and everyone laughed at his jokes. Because of the news, D'Mari put the meeting on hold and told the guys briefly about an idea that he had thought would be a good way to clean up money. J.R. let them know that Lexi's club would be a good place also. The guys talked shit and drank until it was time for J.R. to head out and catch his flight.

11

Once J.R. and his cousins left, Corey felt his phone vibrate in his pocket like it had been doing since he abruptly ended his call when D'Mari walked in. Knowing who it was, he grabbed his phone out of his pocket and answered.

"What?" he sighed deeply.

"I'm not gonna keep fucking playing with ya ass nigga. You think you the fuck slick with that stunt you pulled, but you won't be able to duck me forever nigga. I gave you an opportunity to run me my fucking money in full and you only gave me half bitch! You got forty-eight hours to get me my fucking money or I'm taking everything, and I do mean *every-thing* the fuck from you!"

The call ended, and Corey was on the verge of panic. The warning that he just received was something he couldn't take lightly. Since his car had been shot up a couple of days ago, he knew it was only a matter of time until his new enemy wanted him dead. Corey began to pace the floor and needed something to calm his nerves. His *perks* were stashed at the crib, so alcohol was the next best thing. Grabbing a new bottle of Jack Daniel's, Corey cracked it open, taking huge swig from the bottle. Corey carried the bottle over to the chair he was sitting in earlier and let the alcohol kick in. Taking another swig from the bottle, he pondered on what to do about the threatening phone call he received and the twenty racks that he owed. Corey knew shit would go a lot smoother if he just asked his cousin for help but his pride kicked in.

Finishing off the bottle, Corey grunted as his phone began to ring in his hand. Through his blurred vision, he saw that it was Alyssa calling and sighed before answering the phone.

"Wassup Alyssa?" he tried not to slur his words.

"I didn't know your gathering with J.R and ya cousins was going to take so long," she huffed.

"We're wrapping up now, Lyssa."

"Why the fuck are lying Corey?"

"What?"

"I just texted my sisters and they told me the twins were already home. So where the fuck are you?"

"Look, something came up that I need to handle. I'll be there when I get there aight!"

"I swear on everything I love Corey, if ya ass is cheating on me—"

Corey hung the phone up before she could finish her sentence and turned his phone off. He knew it was only a matter of time before she started talking that cheating bull-shit, and Corey didn't have time for the shit, even though he was the blame for her feeling like that. Since she allowed him back into their bedroom, Corey had been keeping his word and being there for his wife whenever she needed him until his truck was destroyed. He hated that he had to keep shit from his wife, but he didn't have a choice.

Corey sat in the silent building for nearly three hours in a zombie like state as he contemplated his options on how to handle Lue. The safest thing for him to do was to pay the money and move on but that shit didn't sit right with him. He felt like if he paid the money, he'd feel like a bitch; and if kept ducking Lue, Corey would be viewed as a bitch. He grew angry with himself for allowing another nigga to have power over him. With the alcohol fueling his final decision and the courage to execute his plan, he jumped up from the couch, secured the building, hopped in his black Lincoln Navigator with the tinted windows, and peeled out of the driveway with screeching tires. Corey drove over to the West End with Lil' Scrappy's 'No Problems' blasting through his speakers as he sped down the expressway. Getting off at his exit, he turned the music down as he drove to the Budget Inn where Lue and his henchmen watched over the prostitutes they pimped. Corey killed the lights on his car before parking on the corner of the block. He opened his glove compartment, snatched out the ski mask, and reached under the seat for his sub machine gun, making sure it was loaded. Without hesitation, Corey hopped out the truck with engine still running. As soon as his Timberland boots hit the parking lot, he opened fire and didn't care who was out there. The innocent civilians scattered while others dropped like flies. When the parking lot was empty, Corey ceased fire and scanned the parking lot. Seconds later, he spotted Lue and two others rushing out the door of the motel and sent shots in their direction, causing them to hit the ground instantly. With a smile on his face, he jogged back to his truck, jumped in, and pulled off.

The sounds of a couple arguing caused Corey to stir in his sleep.

"Ahhh shit!" he shouted, grabbing his pounding head.

Squeezing his eyes closed, Corey slowly opened his eyes and took in his surroundings through the dark tint. When he realized he was parked a few houses away from his crib, he was confused as to why and wondered what he'd done the night before. The last thing he recalled was drinking in the warehouse last night and the rest was unclear. When Corey noticed the ski mask and the gun on the passenger's side floor, he began to think the worst. He started the engine, backed out of his neighbor's driveway, and headed to his own place. Pulling up in his driveway, Corey cut the engine and sat there, trying to piece together what happen the night before. Gabbing his cell phone out of his pocket, he turned it on and punched in the code. Message after message came through his phone along with a few voicemails from Alyssa. As he viewed the last text from his wife, a call came through from D'Mani.

"Yo cuz?" he answered groggily.

"Nigga!" Corey heard two voices shout in unison. He knew that D'Mari was with him. "What the fuck man!"

"Wassup?"

"Wassup? Wassup? Nigga ya wife came to my crib at fucking three in the morning in a panic," D'Mari responded. "Where the fuck were you last night?"

"When y'all left, I stayed back and had a few more drinks. Lyssa called talking some bullshit about me cheating and I banged on her. I had some shit on my mind last night and didn't feel like hearing that shit. So, I turned my phone off. I was so drunk that I don't know how I made it home. I fell asleep in my truck and just woke up not too long ago," he explained.

"Look man, I understand if you're still fucked up about Boosie, but you gotta stay focused out here nigga," D'Mani replied. "We all got our own personal shit we're dealing with, but we managed to stay on our shit and you need to do the same."

"I hear you cuz," Corey sighed.

"Look, handle ya business with ya wife and meet up with us later," D'Mari added.

"Aight later."

Ending the call, Corey went back to reading the last text from his wife telling him to meet her at the doctor's office by one that afternoon.

"Fuck!" he shouted when saw that it was ten minutes to one.

Jumping out the truck, Corey rushed in the house, took a quick shower, threw on some clothes and sneakers, and dashed out the door. After doing 85mph, he managed to make it to the doctor's office by 1:40pm and saw Alyssa walking out of the door. Parking in the first spot he saw, Corey got out the car with the engine running.

"Alyssa," he called as he approached.

She didn't even look in his direction. Alyssa ignored him, unlocking the doors to her car.

"Alyssa, baby, wait." He pulled on the driver's side door to stop her from closing it.

"Let go of my fucking door Corey!"

"Alyssa, I'm sorry I missed the appointment. I was---"

"You were what huh? At work?"

"Yeah," he hesitantly answered.

"You fucking liar!" Alyssa threw her Snapple bottle at him that missed his head by inches.

"What are you talking about Alyssa?"

"I called the fucking TV station where you work and they told me you *quit* months ago! All this time, I blame myself for tripping on you because I thought you were working hard and shit... but in reality, ya ass is running around here doing God knows what!" Alyssa threw her hair brush at him, hitting him in the chest.

"Alyssa, baby—"

"Fuck you Corey! And don't bring ya ass to my fucking house. You can sleep where ever ya ass slept at last night!"

Yanking the door out of his hands, Alyssa slammed it shut, started her car, and drove off. Corey stood there in the dumb nigga stance until Alyssa was out of sight. He ignored the stares of the people who overheard the conversation with his wife as he walked back to his truck. Closing the door, Corey laid his back on the chair and rubbed his forehead with hand. The headache he woke with had grown into a migraine. Corey was pissed that Alyssa found out that he was no longer working at ESPN and that he was caught in one of the many lies that he had told over the months. He knew that his wife was just speaking out of anger when she said not to come back home and decided that he would give her a couple of days to cool off before he tried to talk to her.

Sitting up, Corey got ready to back out of the lot when a story about a shooting caught his ear. He turned the radio up and listened as the reporter stated that seven people were found dead in the parking lot of the Budget Inn in West End Atlanta and two people were injured. When Corey heard that Lue was one of the victims that was found dead, he smirked. The reporter went on to say that the shooter was still at large and there were no suspects. Glancing down at the ski mask and gun on the floor, a knot grew in his stomach.

"Did I--- Nah. I couldn't have done that shit," Corey shook his head.

His disbelief was unsettling. Corey removed the magazine from the gun and noticed that it was empty. Shoving the gun under the seat, he backed out of the spot and pulled off. His heart pounded out of his chest as he drove down the expressway. *Did I really kill seven people? Is this who I am now? Why the fuck can't I remember what happened last night?* Were just a few questions that ran through Corey's head. For Corey, the thought of pulling the trigger scared him and gave him sense of satisfaction at the same time. In his mind, if he did killed those people, that was his first time pulling the trigger and he was pretty sure that it wouldn't be the last.

12

D'Mani prepared himself to meet up with Cheyanne and Imani and was nervous as fuck. It would be his first time formally being introduced to her, and all he could think about was whether she would like him or not. Outside of Kyler, the only experience he had with kids was the few times he'd held his brother's twins and as small as they were, he never did that often. As much of a thug as he was, nothing had ever pumped fear in him like the thought of baby girl giving him the cold shoulder; and why wouldn't she when his ass was basically a stranger.

"Hmph, you sure are taking a long ass time to get dressed to meet a toddler. Turn around, let me make sure your print ain't showing." Anastasia came into their bedroom, disturbing his thoughts. D'Mani glanced down at the black Champion hoodie and joggers he wore with his fresh all white Ones and frowned. He started to tell her that as big as his dick was, his print showed no matter what he was wearing; but when he turned around, he got too irritated to even joke with her ass. She was standing next to her vanity in a black Balenciaga bodysuit with the word printed all over it and some black high-wasted jeans. Her freshly manicured feet showed through her peep toe booties and her hair was full of thick ass curls. If it had been just a regular date, D'Mani would have been canceling that shit, so they could stay in. That's how good she looked, but under the circumstances, it was way too much.

"Stasia, I got on some old regular ass shit... you the one dressed like you bouta go to fashion week."

"I dress like this all the time," she lied easily and went to spray some of her Prada perfume on.

D'Mani dropped the conversation, knowing there was no win. For one, she knew they were meeting them at the Children's Museum, so dressing up was unnecessary; and for two, she'd already been in a nasty mood since he told her that he wasn't getting a DNA test. That shit had started a whole nother argument and she'd basically been giving him the silent treatment ever since. When he told her about him and Cheyanne meeting so that he could spend time with Imani, she immediately invited herself. D'Mani had never seen her act so insecure the entire time they'd been together, but the last thing he wanted was to make her feel as if she needed to compete with any female on earth, so he'd allowed her to come. Now, he was seeing that she only wanted to be there to size up Cheyanne and try to outdo her. D'Mani didn't want her to feel anymore threatened than she already did, so he elected not to tell her that Cheyanne wasn't out to take her spot. Though he'd never been in a situation like the one he was currently in, he knew women enough to know that it was taboo to *"take up"* for another woman.

An hour later, they were walking inside of the spacious museum after paying at the door. D'Mani spotted Cheyanne right away dressed down in a gray Champions sweatshirt and jogger set similar to his with black Pumas covering her small feet. Her hair was in a sloppy bun on top of her head and her face looked bare of any makeup, but she was just as gorgeous as ever. She started in their direction with Imani tagging along beside her with a huge grin.

"What the fuck?" He heard Stasia hiss under her breath and he could feel her eyes on him ready to cut up. "Let me find out."

"It's nothing to find out man. She obviously dressed for the occasion, nothin' more nothin' less. Don't try and read more into this than it is Anastasia. I'm just tryna get to know Imani," D'Mani warned through clenched teeth, still smiling as they approached.

"Hmph! Let you tell it. Getting to know Imani *better be all* yo ass doin-"

"Hey! You guys made it!" Cheyanne said excitedly once she came to a stop in front of them. "I'm Cheyanne, and this lil cutie is Imani." She stuck out a hand to Anastasia and wrapped her other arm around Imani's shoulder. In true diva mode, Stasia barely placed her hand inside of Cheyanne's as she gave her a phony smile. Unsure of what to make of her attitude, Cheyanne looked to D'Mani with a puzzled expression, but he was just as confused as she was, so he set his attention on his daughter.

"Hi Imani, did your mama tell you who I am?" he asked, kneeling down so that they were eye level. She grinned at him shyly and shook her head *no*.

"I *already* know who you is."

"*Are* Mani, I already know who you are," Cheyanne corrected.

"I know who you *are*," Imani huffed with an eye roll. "My daddy right, and this yo girlfriend?" She briefly looked at Anastasia who gave her a small wave.

"That's right... I am your daddy and this is my girlfriend, Stasia."

"She pretty!" she giggled, covering her mouth with both hands.

"Aww thank you!" Stasia gushed.

"*She's* pretty Imani," Cheyanne told her at the same time. D'Mani loved how she corrected her speech so that she would grow up talking properly. It was one of the ways he knew he was blessed in the baby mama department. Out of all the females he'd ever laid with, Cheyanne would have been his ideal choice to reproduce with. She was smart, beautiful, and apparently a good mother from what he saw.

"Yeah she is pretty huh.. Do you mind if me and her spend some time here with you and yo mama?" he asked, taking in how smart and polite she was.

"Yeah, come on!" she dropped her mother's hand and immediately grabbed ahold of D'Mani and Stasia's, pulling them toward the first station. He looked back to see that Cheyanne was smiling with appreciation as she followed them over, staying back a small ways to allow him time with her. She didn't seem bothered at all by Anastasia being there or being involved and he hoped that Stasia noticed it too.

They spent a couple hours playing around at the different stations, and after a while, it seemed like Anastasia had loosened up and began to enjoy herself; though that may have been because Cheyanne was giving them a wide range of space. It was obvious her feet were aching from walking around in those heels, but he'd tried to warn her. Now they were sitting off to the side resting while Imani was in the play area with the other kids.

Cheyanne came over and sat with them and it seemed like Stasia's already tight face grew tighter, letting him know that her attitude was back with her presence. He figured that even though she was being childish, at least her attitude was about Cheyanne and not his damn daughter cause that would have been a straight deal breaker. He hoped that once she realized

Cheyanne was nothing more than an old friend and his child's mother that her icy behavior would thaw out.

"Y'all tired yet?" Cheyanne joked, joining them on one of the many benches that were there for the parents to watch the kids.

"Hell yeah! I ain't know toddlers had that much energy," D'Mani admitted, pointing to Imani who was running around with another little girl. "And she still goin'!"

"Yeah this is pretty much how she is from 7 a.m. until she goes to bed at night." The two shared a laugh and then fell into an uncomfortable silence before she spoke again. "Look, I apologize again about keeping this from you, and I appreciate you, both of you," she looked between him and Anastasia. "for accepting Imani."

"It's nothin' to accept, she's *mine*, so she's family," he cut her off, intertwining his hand inside of Stasia's, ignoring how her body stiffened, and she let her hand sit loosely inside of his.

"That's great... she was starting to ask about you, and honestly, all I could do was show her old pictures because I didn't even know how to get in contact with you. I'm glad we ended up running into each other at Wal-Mart of all places."

"Yeah, me too ma."

Tears glistened in her eyes as she turned her attention back to Imani. Anastasia dug her fingernails into D'Mani's hand with a plastic smile on her face.

"Wrap this shit up and let's go. I'm goin' to the car. I can't take another minute of y'all skinnin' and grinnin' in each other face," she whispered under her breath and stood up to leave before he could say anything. Unsure of what had happened, Cheyanne looked at him with confusion written all over her face.

"She got an important call to make, but we should really be heading out anyway," he lied, glancing at the Audemar on his wrist. She gave him a *nigga please* look but he wasn't about to change his story. Even though on the inside he was pissed off at how childish Stasia was being, he wasn't going to ever paint her in a bad light; but he was *definitely* about to go check her. Him and Cheyanne hadn't given her any reason to think that there was more going on than them coming together for Imani, so her rude behavior was uncalled for; and honestly, it had him looking at her funny.

"Okayyyyy, well let me call Imani over to say bye," she dragged out still looking unsure of his explanation, but still dropping it, calling Imani over. Her little head popped up and he could hear her beads clicking as she ran to them.

"Did you see me jumpin'?" she asked, bouncing into her dad's arms. Over the course of the day, she'd gotten considerably closer to him, and it was a good feeling knowing that his baby girl took a liking to him off the bat.

"I did, you was killin' that shi-, stuff." He stopped himself from cursing since she'd been telling him it was bad to curse all day. "Daddy gotta head home though, but I'll be to see you again later this week?" he asked, locking eyes with Cheyanne who nodded that he could.

"Can I go too? I wanna meet Kyler!"

"Ummm... not tonight Mani, maybe next time."

She pouted up at her mother, but didn't argue after seeing the look on her face. *Cheyanne must not play when it comes to whining,* D'Mani noted. "Yeah, what yo mama said, and I'll make sure I have a bunch of snacks to eat and games to play... it can be a big sleepover," he added, causing her to giggle as he tickles her belly.

It took another fifteen minutes before she finally let him go and he made it out to the car where Stasia was fuming. Just like he'd been doing pretty much the whole day, he ignored her and headed home to drop her off and check in with his traps. They were still new and he occasionally popped in to make sure niggas was doing what they were supposed to.

"So, we just gone skip over how you were just all in each other's faces back there?" she finally asked after they were close to home.

"Yep, cause we wasn't in each other's face, that's yo ass seein' shit that ain't there!" D'Mani snapped loudly. He had hoped that it would be something they could talk about once they got home, but her attitude and snippy ass comments had finally took him there. "This shit ain't about *you*, it ain't even about me and Cheyanne! It's about me getting to know *my* kid, and instead of *you* being there for *me* like *I* was for *you*, you wanna throw fits and act an ass like I did something wrong! I didn't fuckin' *know* Stasia!" She looked at him stunned at the tone he was using and his choice of words like she hadn't been asking for it.

"So, now I'm wrong for havin' feelin's... bet yo ass ain't snap on that bitch when she came outta nowhere with a damn 3 year old claiming its yours!" she clapped back, rolling her neck as they pulled in front of their house. D'Mani didn't know what else he could say to get her to understand where he was coming from, and he wasn't in the mood to go back and forth with her anymore that night.

"Mann, take yo ass in the house Anastasia," he sighed, done with the conversation.

"No, we're not fini-"

"Get the *fuck* out Stasia damn!" he barked, cutting her off and causing her to jump out of the car. He pulled off before she could close the door good, punching the steering wheel angrily.

D'Mani was so mad that he wasn't paying any attention to his surroundings. Twenty minutes later when he pulled up to the first trap on his agenda, he didn't even notice the black SUV that had been following him. Shots rang out as he started up the walkway, and he managed to make it up to the porch before a bullet entered his leg, sending him down.

A bunch of armed niggas ran out of the house and started shooting at the truck, but they were already disappearing around the corner and he was losing consciousness. He could hear his team standing over him arguing over what to do when he finally succumbed to the darkness.

13

"Would the lovely parents like to know the sex of the baby?" the young ultrasound tech asked, briefly looking up from the monitor at J.R. and Lexi.

"Yeah," J.R. blurted out first.

"*Hell no!* I mean no," Lexi sounded off behind him.

J.R. shot her a look, awaiting an explanation and that's exactly what he got.

"Baby, I want to have a gender reveal party and...."

"Lexi, don't nobody got time for all that shit," he stated, cutting her off in mid-sentence.

"Well this is *my* first child and I don't care what YOU have time for. I want to be so surprised, so ma'am, thank you but no thanks. You can place the results in a sealed envelope and I will give it to one of my sisters. Thank you," she snapped, taking the paper towel and wiping the excess gel off of her stomach.

J.R. stood to his feet but didn't say another word. Lexi's attitude on top of all the other shit he was dealing with was too much stress on him at the time. All he wanted to do was go to the crib and smoke a blunt but that seemed to be asking for too much. After scheduling her next appointment, the couple headed to the car but not before Lexi started with the twenty-one questions.

"You talk to D'Mani?" she quizzed.

"Yeah, this morning Alexis before you got up. He's good," he further explained.

"Sooooooo, how the fuck he just move here and got niggas shooting at him already Jeremy?" she inquired.

"I was in Philly, I have no idea Alexis," he replied nonchalantly as he turned onto the street.

"Nigga, you so full of shit. Y'all got some shit going on in these streets J.R., and I just want to make sure that my son or daughter have their father around," she spoke softly, rubbing her small hardened stomach.

J.R.'s eyes shifted from the road to her and then back at the road again before he too placed his hand on her stomach.

"I love y'all man, ain't shit gon' happen. I ain't gon' lie, we might have gotten ourselves into some shit but trust and believe, you and my baby will always be straight," J.R. replied sincerely.

His words must have been enough to ease Lexi's mind temporarily because they rode the rest of the ride in silence. Hearing about D'Mani being shot, whether it was the leg or not, still didn't sit right with him. He wondered if it was the young boys under Dex sending a message or even Tessa himself. J.R. knew that he needed to get a hold on shit sooner than later and it was time to start putting the plan in motion, especially since he had a family to protect.

Pulling up to their home almost an hour later, J.R. helped his girl out of the car and headed into the house. As soon as he opened the door, loud music greeted them, the sounds of

Yo Gotti blasted through their normally quiet home. J.R. glanced over at Lexi who rolled her eyes and headed towards the music. He watched as she snatched the remote control out of the bar, completely muting it.

"We need to have a talk cuz this shit not gon' work." She smacked her lips while slipping out of her Nikes.

Instead of replying, he called out to Yasmine, who came running down the stairs a few minutes later in a tank top and small shorts. J.R. had to do a double take at his baby sister who was shaped and dressed like a grown woman.

"What up bro?" she spoke, smacking on the piece of gum that was in her mouth.

"Why the fuck you got this music blasting like this?" he asked, looking around the living at her belongings that was scattered everywhere.

"My bad... I didn't know y'all was gon' be home so soon," she replied, looking over at Lexi who remained quiet.

"Aight look, we need to set some ground rules around *if* you are going to be living with us," he stated.

"Living with us? Look, handle this down here and I'll be upstairs. You need to holler at me," Lexi finally chimed in before walking off.

Had J.R. only thought before he spoke, he would have had a better chance at handling the situation. After the passing of his mom, J.R. took his only sibling and brought her back to Atlanta with him. He told Lexi it was temporary, but he lied; he knew he wasn't going to send Yasmine back to Philly without real supervision.

"I guess yo lil girlfriend not happy with me being here," Yas stated, rolling her eyes and flopping down on the couch.

"Watch yo mouth and respect my shit," he replied, knocking her feet off of his leather couch.

"I know I'm not ma but shit gon' run the same way. You

need to apply for some colleges and start school. As long as you in school, you won't have to want for shit but don't think you finna be out here playing Yasmine," he scolded.

"I knoooooow brother, but I miss her already," she replied in a somber tone.

J.R. walked over and took a seat next to his baby sister.

"I miss her too, but we got each other. I just need you to stay focus," he reminded her.

J.R. hugged Yasmine before making his way upstairs to handle Lexi. He knew it wasn't going to be easy, but he knew how to handle her by now. He knew her mouth could be reckless at times, but she meant no harm.

When J.R. entered the room, Lexi was laying in the bed, scrolling through her phone. He walked straight up to her and snatched it. She shot him a look that could kill but kept her mouth closed.

"I know I told you the living situation with Yasmine was temporarily, but it's not looking too good," he confessed, taking a seat at the foot of the bed.

"What you mean not looking too good?" she quizzed, sitting up in the bed.

"I'm *not* sending her back to Philly with my aunt... she'll let Yas run wild," He explained.

"Ok, I get that... but neither you nor I know nothing about raising a teenager. Hell, we were just teenagers ourselves a few years ago baby," she replied.

Lexi was right, they were only twenty-two themselves; they had no idea how to raise Yas.

"On some real shit, we don't have a choice. I know my mother would want that," he explained.

"Well, say less. We gon' wing this shit together, but Yasmine needs to realize that it's only one big momma in this house," she stated, poking her lips out for a kiss.

J.R. took the invitation and kissed her full lips before

hugging her. The talk went better than he thought. He just began to wonder how the fuck was he going to run his household, raise a teenager, and deal with the hormones of his pregnant girlfriend, all the while dodging bullets in the streets.

🎋 14 🎋

It took D'Mari an hour to make it to his destination out in Suwanne, but he was ahead of time, which meant he was on time in his book. He sat there for a few minutes reading over some documents and killed the engine when Corey pulled up about ten minutes later. D'Mari was just about to hit him up asking where he was, but he put his phone in his briefcase and got out after putting his suit jacket on. Mari got out with the intentions of speaking and dapping his cousin up, but his words got caught somewhere in his throat as he stared at Corey who was dressed in some jeans and a USPA shirt.

"Nigga what the fuck you got on and where the fuck you find a... never mind. You gotta change or Ima just handle this shit by myself," Mari spat and shook his head.

He had been feeling like Corey had some shit going on, but it was no longer a thought. The vision before him proved that something was terribly wrong.

"What's wrong wit what I got on?" Corey challenged as he ran his hands down over his outfit.

"Are you high? What the fuck goin' on wit you man?"

"Mari... you know damn well I don't smoke. Come on and let's go handle this business," Corey urged while looking around.

"Bruh, just wait in the truck until I finish," Mari instructed and began to walk off.

"I can't... I'll just come in and go to the bathroom to stay outta the way," Corey pleaded.

When Mari turned around, he noticed that Corey was still looking around like someone may have been following him. Something inside told him to just allow his cousin to go in with him so that was what he did. Mari had already made up his mind that as soon as they finished handling their business, he was going to have a good ass talk with his cousin to find out what the fuck he really had going on.

"Good morning. I'm here for a meeting with Mr. Sampson," Mari spoke to the receptionist with the long blonde weave.

"You must be Mr. Mitchell?" she smiled.

"I am," he kept it cordial.

"He's expecting to you. Just have a seat and if there's anything I can do to make you more comfortable, just let me know."

Mari nodded his head and took that as his opportunity to step back and wait. He was meeting with Mr. Sampson about a trucking business. After doing a shit load of research of his own, Mari had pretty much learned the ins and outs already, the only thing he needed an inside connect for was for a list of independent drivers. Once he retrieved that list, the rest would be up to him to contact drivers and negotiate. If shit went right, they would have the best of both worlds. Not only would they be able to clean their money up, they would also be able to transport drugs without being detected.

Corey had managed to stay out of dodge and an hour later, Mari was trailing behind him on the way to one of the trap houses. The business meeting had gone better than expected, and he had already texted the boyz and let them know that shit was about to be on and poppin' in the A. Mari drove in silence as he contemplated what he wanted to say and how he wanted to say it to his cousin. Being with Drea had taught him a little about thinking shit through. Being that Corey was his cousin and brother, he knew that he had to approach the situation differently anyway; but no matter what, he had to find out what the fuck was going on. The ringing of Mari's phone interrupted his thoughts. If it wouldn't have been Drea's ringtone, he would have let the call go to voicemail.

"What's up bae?"

"What the fuck wrong wit yo cousin? Ima fuck him up for stressing my sister out while she pregnant and shit. I'll fuck his light bright ass all the way up," Drea ranted.

"Babe he ain't even all that brig..."

"Oh so you taking up for him? Ain't that bout a..."

"Drea naw... calm down. I'm actually bout to talk to Corey now. I honestly don't know what's goin' on, but I'm gon' get to the bottom of it. What Lyssa say?"

"I'll tell you after you find out what he got to say. My next appointment just arrived. I'll call you later. Bye."

D'Mari couldn't do shit but shake his head at his wife. He knew all too well how the Holiday sisters operated. Those girls would literally try to fight some dudes if it came down to it. A few minutes later, Mari turned onto the street of the first trap house they had established. He saw the shit about to happen and reached for his gun as soon as shots rang out at Corey's truck. Mari fired off round after round after round. He hit the back window of the black Jeep Cherokee, but it kept going. After parking abruptly, he ran up to his cousin's truck and saw nothing but blood.

"I'm... I'm.. sor..."

"Don't try to talk man. I got you," Mari tried to remain calm, but on the inside, he was fucked up.

"Don't close your eyes," he pleaded with Corey, but he it was pointless because Corey closed his eyes. Mari put him in the passenger's seat and hauled ass towards the hospital. He didn't have time for a street doctor.

✺ 15 ✺

After being in the hospital for nearly forty eight hours, Corey was more than grateful that he survived the shooting that came damn close to ending his life. With all the rounds that were fired at his truck, he was only shot four times, two shots in the chest, neck, and ribs. The doctors surgically removed all four of the bullets. Corey came close to losing his life on the operating table due to the amount of blood he lost. Spending fourteen hours in sedation, when he came to, Corey was beyond happy to see his wife right there by his side. He apologized numerous times for his behavior, the , and the pain that he'd put her through. Corey was glad that his wife had forgiven him with ease. He was tired of them being at odds behind his bullshit.

When the sun came up the next morning, Corey had been up for twelve hours straight and as tired as he was, he couldn't sleep for shit. Everything that he had done over the past few months while he was sober or intoxicated hit him all at once and it finally broke him. It was time for him to admit that his ass had a serious problem. Not only to himself but to his brothers as well. Around eight that morning, Corey received a text from D'Mari telling him that him and his brothers would be there to see him at nine. He replied okay and waited for them to arrive.

"Nah Baby, I'm good. Go head and go to work and I'll see you later on," Corey spoke to his wife on Facetime.

"Are you sure? You know Drea will understand if I have to call out."

"Yes, I'm sure. Plus my brother are coming so I'll be good," he assured her as he washed his face.

"Have you thought about what we talked about Corey?"

Corey's jaw got tight as he thought back to the conversation they had about him going to rehab. When the doctor informed her that he had a large amount of alcohol and drugs in his system that day D'Mari rushed him to the hospital, Alyssa expressed her concerns about his drinking and drug habits.

"Yeah, I have and to be honest, I'm not feeling it, Lyssa," Corey answered irritably.

"Why ain't you feeling it? Because you think people are gonna talk about you and call you an addict or a junkie?"

Corey stared at her on the screen.

"Look, I know that this is a difficult subject for you to discuss but ya ass need to face facts, okay? You have a serious problem Corey and you need help."

"Yo cuz?" He heard his cousin call out.

"Yo. I'll be out in a minute."

"Lyssa, I gotta go. Can we talk about this later?"

"Think about what I said Corey. I love you."

"I Love you too."

Ending the call, Corey finished up in the bathroom and greeted his brothers with handshakes when he came out. The looks displayed on his cousins and J.R. face told him that they were pissed about something and he was sure that they were going to let him know why.

"How you feeling man?" D'Mari questioned.

"I'm still a lil sore but I'll be coming home in a couple of days," Corey nodded his head.

"I didn't think ya ass was going to make it at first man. It was touch and go for a minute," D'Mani spoke. "But best believe a nigga was glad when they said ya ass was gonna pull through my nigga."

"These niggas getting a little too bold. It's time we boss up on these motherfuckas. They caught Mani in the leg and now they got C laid up in the hospital. This shit has to end," J.R. let his anger be known.

"I agree but there is something I gotta ask you first Corey?" D'Mari darted his eyes at his cousin.

"Wassup?"

"That shooting, was it related to the shit we doing or was that about something else? I've been thinking back to how you were when you showed up for our meeting and how paranoid you were. If you got yaself involved in some shit, you need to let us know *right the fuck now*."

Corey glanced around at his family and knew that it was time for him to come clean. Preparing himself for whatever was to come, he spoke.

"When we first moved out here, my partner I worked with took me to a gambling spot in West Atlanta, and after I quit my job, I still continued to go. I told myself that I was only gonna go a couple of times a month, but the more I won, the more I went. My addiction for gambling and winning had got the best me, and I ended up being damn near $30,000 in debt to the nigga that ran the spot. Not being able to deal with the shit, I started drinking and popping *perks* something heavy. To the point where I wouldn't remember what I did after I took them. The night of our meeting, I killed the

84

nigga Lue, the nigga I owed money to and a few other people that night. That shit that happened the other day was out of retaliation of that. I'm not sure if the shooters are the same as Mani's though. I know I coulda told y'all what was up but my pride wouldn't let me," Corey confessed.

The room was dead silent and the expressions that his brothers wore on their faces caused his heart rate to increase.

"Hold the fuck up! So you telling us that all this shit is behind a gambling debt, C?" D'Mani spoke through gritted teeth.

"Yeah."

"Did you give that nigga anything?" J.R.

"Yeah...the money that was missing... I took it to pay Lue."

Without warning, D'Mani lunged towards Corey, but Mari and J.R. held him back.

"Nigga, do you know what *the fuck* you did? Huh?" Mani shouted.

"Mani calm down and come on!" J.R. dragged Mani out the room.

Corey watched as D'Mari paced the floor in frustration. On the outside, his demeanor was calm, but he was shitting bricks on the inside. Corey was aware of his betrayal and knew how his cousins handled niggas that were disloyal to them. But being as though he was family, he didn't know what the fuck to expect.

"D'Mari, man, I'm sorry."

"Shut the fuck up, man! *Sorry* ain't gonna *undo* none of the shit you did my nigga. Not only did you lie to us but you *framed* ya homie for some shit he didn't do. Instead of opening ya fucking mouth, you let this shit go on to the point where you killed a nigga and didn't even give us a heads up. You got us thinking that this shit is all related to one thing, but ya ass done got up in some silly shit," Mari shook his head. "I thought I knew you better than that, and if I woulda known that this lifestyle was gonna have ya like this, I woulda told ya ass to keep ya 9-5."

Silence filled the room once again.

"So what's gonna happen to me now?" Corey asked moments later.

"I don't know but ya ass is on the bench until further notice," Mari spoke sternly.

"What you mean I'm on *the bench*?"

"That means you can't make no moves until you get ya shit together. Respect is *earned*. Not *given* and I *lost* respect for you. I got niggas I've known for years working with us that never crossed me. I never thought that my own family would," he glanced at Corey with disappointment. "I'll hit you up in a few days, man."

When his cousin left out the room, Corey remained on the edge of the hospital bed deep in thought. The weight was finally lifted of his shoulders, but the *guilt* of his actions was heavy on his heart. Corey valued his family even though they may have thought otherwise because of the bullshit he'd brought their way. Hearing his cousin tell him that all he had to do was speak up was easier said than done for Corey. What man wanted to ask another man for help solving an issue that didn't concern him? Pride allowed Corey to dig hole too deep for him to climb out of, but he wasn't going to allow his pride to keep him there. Grabbing his phone, he googled some rehab centers in the area and called a few. The fact that his ass had been benched didn't sit well with him, but Corey understood why D'Mari made that decision. Although he fucked up in a major way, Corey had to do whatever was needed to fix shit with his family.

16

D 'Mani limped out of his house in a hurry, ignoring the sound of Anastasia in the background yelling. He didn't care where he was going; he just needed to put some distance between them. It seemed like ever since he told her about Imani, she was always fucking mad. He thought he would gain a little act right from her because of his injury, but her ass wasn't cutting him no slack; and if anything, she was on his back even more.

They'd just gotten into for the third time that day alone because he told Kyler to let him get some shuteye before they played the game together. Ever since he'd gotten shot, his leg would get to acting up on him, and the pain pills he was on had him tired as hell whenever he did take them, which was the case. Did Anastasia understand that though? Hell nah! While Kyler went on about his business and found something else to do like any normal person would have, Anastasia went crazy. She went into the living room where he had just closed his eyes asking him *if he would have told his daughter that he would play later?*

Despite being dog ass tired, he sat right up and gave her a

death stare, glad that Kyler had left out of the room, so he didn't hear that bullshit came out her mouth. Before he could even say anything, she started going in, yelling about how he'd been treating Kyler funny ever since he found out about Imani. He was completely shocked by the accusation, but he wasn't about to argue with her goofy ass. Not when he was drowsy as hell and still in pain.

Fighting off the slight fog he was in, he slipped on his slides, snatched up his car keys, and hobbled away not, even grabbing the crutches that he was supposed to be using. With his phone in one hand and his keys in the other, he dialed up his brother, getting the voicemail twice before making it to the car. It was probably best for him NOT to go to any house that her sisters resided in, considering that would be the first place she looked for him. Mani already knew that she would have them geeked up with her paranoia. Corey's bullshit made him REALLY not even consider calling him. His ass had everybody conflicted as fuck.

His best bet would be a hotel; at least there, he would get some quiet to sleep so that he could prepare to tear the streets up behind the shooting. He didn't have a clue of which henchman that Tessa had sent after him, but he was for damn sure planning to find out... as soon as he got some rest.

D'Mani had reached the corner by the time he realized that he left his wallet, but there was no way he was going back to get it. Stasia probably wouldn't let him back out and he damn sure ain't wanna stay there with her.

Ten minutes later, fighting his heavy lids and out of options, he found himself pulling to a stop in front of Cheyanne's crib. He chastised himself for coming to the person that was unintentionally wreaking havoc on his life. However, he knew if he didn't pull over soon, he would have been falling asleep at the wheel. He'd recently found out that she lived right in the next neighborhood over. Stepping out of the car, he had to stop and lean against it, due to a wave of dizziness hitting him.

"Shit!"

D'Mani closed his eyes, hoping that the spell would pass. After a few seconds, it did, giving him the chance to make his way to her front door. He hadn't seen her car in the driveway, but he was hoping that maybe she had parked in the garage. After pressing the doorbell, he almost instantly heard Imani bouncing around inside and shrieking, bringing a brief smile to his face.

"Imani you better sit back down and finish eating!" Cheyanne yelled before the locks began to turn and the door was swung open. "Uhhh hey D'Mani. What you doin' here?" she asked with an uncomfortable look on her face. He realized that he didn't know if she lived with someone or not. For some reason, the thought bothered him, but he tried not to let it show.

"I was in the neighborhood and figured I'd stop through and check y'all out," he lied and gave her a lazy grin, hoping to put her at ease about his visit. She looked past him as if she thought Anastasia would pop out of the bushes before waving him in.

"Okay well, we were just having dinner. Did you eat?" she moved back a bit to allow him in and then closed the door behind him.

"Naw, I'm straight," he declined, following her through the foyer and into the back of the house where he figured they were eating. D'Mani took in the traditional style she was going for and nodded in approval of how homey and clean the place was. He had always known her to be a clean and organized person, so it was no surprise that even with a toddler, things hadn't changed.

"Guess who came to see you?" she asked Imani as she

entered the kitchen with him lagging behind. From where he was, D'Mani could see Imani sitting in some kind of booster seat that allowed her to reach the table easily. She smiled up at her mother and shoveled more food into her mouth.

"Hey Mani."

"Daddy!!" she shrieked happily, throwing her arms up for a hug. D'Mani tried to walk over to her normally without alerting Cheyanne of his wound. He grabbed up his baby girl into a hug not, even caring about the spaghetti sauce that she was covered in. "Stoppp!!" she giggled wildly while he tickled her and planted wet kisses on her cheeks. After a minute or two, he put her back in her seat, so she could finish eating before her food got cold while Cheyanne looked on quietly.

Once Imani was back to eating, he turned to face Cheyanne and noticed her staring into space with a slight frown.

"You cool?" he questioned playfully and she blinked before focusing on his face.

"Yeah I'm fine, but are you?" The playful smirk he had slipped from his lips and his brows drew together in confusion. Cheyanne clarified her meaning by nodding at his leg.

"You're bleeding through your jeans." And that's when he realized that she had been looking at his damn leg that whole time. D'Mani glanced down at the blood slowly seeping through his whitewashed Levi's and silently cursed himself for not changing his dressing before he rushed out of the house. The last thing he wanted was for her to think that things were dangerous for him in the streets since that was ultimately what had driven her away with his daughter in the first place.

"Oh that ain't shit, I scraped it on a nail in my basement earlier," he tried to lie, but from the look on her face he could tell she wasn't going for it.

"Imani finish eating while I go get daddy a band aid." She

told their daughter who was still slurping up noodles and making a big mess on the glass table. Imani nodded her understanding through a mouthful and Cheyanne walked out of the kitchen, motioning for him to follow. When they got to the half bathroom that was in the hall, she closed the door slightly and turned to him with a scowl.

"So, are you gone tell me what really happened or you gone continue to lie?"

"Ayite," D'Mani said simply.

"Ayite?"

"Ayite I'm gone tell you." She nodded silently and pointed to the closed toilet seat for him to sit down. After she retrieved the first aid kit from the medicine cabinet, she squatted down to survey the damage.

"You gone have to take these damn pants off, cause for one, you getting blood all over and two, I can't roll them up," Cheyanne huffed finally after struggling for a while at his ankles.

"I got it I-." D'Mani started but she cut him off.

"Obviously you don't or the dressing that's already on there wouldn't be leaking. I'm not trying to make this situation uncomfortable. You know I'm a professional, so stop stalling, drop yo pants and explain nigga," she stood before him with her hands planted on her hips.

D'Mani sighed, but he stood and did as she said, hurrying to sit back down so that she couldn't catch a glimpse of his Versace boxers. She smacked her lips in annoyance at him and pulled his pants off the rest of the way so that she could inspect his wound.

"You got shot?" she asked alarmed, looking up at him.

"Yeah, but this shit don't happen on the regular so don't think that I'd bring any harm to Imani."

"Relax, I'm not planning on keeping her away from you. Although I am slightly concerned about your lifestyle, I'm more worried about you putting so much strain on your leg that its bleeding through," she let him know. He released a sigh, relieved that she wasn't ready to run with his daughter yet again due to his dealings in the streets, trying not to let her concern change the way he viewed their relationship.

"Appreciate that, and as far as this lil shit go," he nodded down towards his leg. "I just been rippin' and runnin', you know...." He trailed off with a shrug. Even though he was into it with Anastasia, he wasn't about to talk down on her to anybody, let alone the source of her frustration. Cheyanne's face showed her disapproval, but she silently got back to work, cleaning him up and before he knew it, she was finished.

"All done," she chimed, standing to her feet.

D'Mani admired her work briefly before nodding his approval.

"Damn thanks nurse Chey,." he called her by the nickname he'd given her years ago.

"That's RN Chey to you nigga," she gloated proudly.

"Aww damn, I see you took it up some notches huh?"

"Yeah, after I found out about Imani, I went and finished school... you know I had to get right for my baby."

D'Mani nodded, realizing that they hadn't really gotten caught up on each other's lives besides where it concerned Imani. He had always known that she was smart. It was good to know that she'd been able to acquire her wealth with her brain unlike a lot of the females he had been seeing lately.

"Well let me throw these in the wash and get Mani down, I'm sure she's looking for us," she said after a long awkward silence had settled over them. She snatched his pants up off the floor preparing to leave the bathroom when he stopped her.

"Aye! I need somethin' to put on, I can't be here like this," he looked down at his bare legs and she let out a laugh.

"Oh shit! My bad......do you got something in the car you can change into cause as you can see, we don't have many men running around here."

"I got a gym bag out there, and it should be some hoopin' shorts in it. My keys in my pockets," he told her and she fished them out quickly.

"Okay be right back."

After Cheyanne came back with his shorts, D'Mani slipped them right on and went to chill in the living room while she gave Imani a bath. He was supposed to be reading her a bedtime story, but as soon as his body settled into the plush couch, his eyes drifted closed and sleep overcame him.

He woke up to the sound of the doorbell being rang repeatedly and his phone vibrating in his lap. The room was now dark and he blinked a few times unsure of where he was as his eyes adjusted to the darkness. *What the fuck?* He realized that he was still at Cheyanne's and it was going on midnight. She probably figured he needed the sleep and didn't want to wake him, which he did; but now he had to deal with the fact that he'd been MIA for hours. His phone started vibrating again and D'Mari's name flashed across the screen. He ignored it quickly, trying to come up with an explanation as he stumbled to the front door to see who was ringing his baby mama shit like that at that time of night. He wasn't on no jealous shit but baby girl was sleep and so was Cheyanne cause she still hadn't gotten up to answer her own door. As soon as he figured out how to get there in the dark, he swung the door open ready to curse somebody out. However, he was surprised to see an irritated D'Mari standing there with his phone to his ear. When he saw D'Mani, the frown he wore deepened and he shoved his phone in his pocket.

"Nigga yo ass done fucked up now!"

❧ 17 ❧

J.R. relaxed on the couch, blunt in one hand and the remote control in the other. He stared at the box that sat on the table in front of him. He read over his mother's name which was written in a black marker on the side. He'd been avoiding going through the paperwork since her passing, but he knew he couldn't avoid it much longer.

"Finally going to give it a look huh?" Lexi appeared out of nowhere and asked, flopping down next to him.

"Yeah, I might as well," he replied, muting the television and sitting up straight.

"I just hate that I never got a chance to meet her while she was alive, but her services was beautiful," she reminisced.

"Yeah, everybody loved my OG and her church family made sure she was good. I just wish....."

J.R. paused when he noticed Yasmine standing in the doorway. He still hadn't had THAT talk with his younger sister, but he figured now was better than never.

"Yas, come here, let me holler at you." He motioned with his hands for her to come and sit down.

Yasmine walked her chubby frame over to him and slowly

sat down. J.R. grabbed her hand and ran his fingers across the ring that rested on her middle finger.

"I bet you'll never take that off huh?" he asked, rubbing his hands over the diamond cut ring.

"Never. It was one of the last things she gave to me," Yas replied in a somber tone.

"Yeah, ma loved that ring. You know Pops gave it to her when he found out she was pregnant with you," he informed her.

Yasmine shook her head up and down as tears flooded her face. J.R. tried his best to stay strong, but it was no good; he too dropped a tear, the first tear since she died. J.R. and his mother Kenya was close. They talked almost every day. He had been trying to get her to move to Atlanta since he'd been there, but she wouldn't budge. Philly was home for her and it was all she knew. Kenya passed away from a brain aneurysm, which was shocking because she was in perfect health. Their father, Peanut, was active in their lives up until Yasmine turned ten. All J.R. remembered was his mother and father arguing. Something was said about his father and an outside child and then it was like Peanut vanished into thin air. Their mother never talked about it; even when they asked questions, she'd change the subject, so they eventually stopped asking.

"I swear, I'll never take it off," she smiled through the tears.

J.R. heard sniffles coming from the right of him. He looked over at Lexi who was crying her eyes out. Through the hard times, she had been right by his side and for that, he was thankful.

"Look, I love y'all, but we gotta stop this mushy shit aight. Man up!" he joked, pulling both of his favorite girls into a hug.

The trio shared a laugh before Yasmine dismissed herself.

J.R. ran his hands over his beard before letting out a frustrating sigh.

"She's a good kid. She'll be ok." Lexi informed him before she too got up and excused herself as well.

Yasmine was in fact a good kid. Everything just happened so unexpectedly and he had no time to prepare. Guess that's the thing about death, you don't see the shit coming.

J.R. sat on the couch a little longer, staring at the box yet again. He was meeting up with his cousin Julian and D'Mari in a few. He figured that their team could use another hard body since they were getting shot at left and right. Julian hustled and ran a few blocks on the Southside, but he was ready to get some real money.

J.R. looked at the box one last time and promised to go through his mother's things at a later date because right now, he had to buss a move. Tossing his all black Champion pullover over his head, he snatched his keys and phone and headed out the door. They were meeting at a bar called Tracy's over East. One of his boys from the block Trigga owned the place. They could grab a bite to eat, along with some drinks, and get shit figured out.

J.R. arrived at the bar and grill about forty minutes later. He shot a text to both guys, and they almost immediately texted back. Julian was pulling up and D'Mani was already inside waiting at a table. J.R. grabbed his .45 out of the glove department, tucked it in his waist, and jumped out. As soon as his white Air Max 95s hit the pavement, Julian came flying in the parking lot like a bat out of hell. He pulled into the spot next to J.R. so fast, he had to rush out of the way.

"Nigga, I ain't gon' hit you," Julian laughed, opening the driver's side door.

"Bitch, I know you ain't but this ain't Philly... these Atlanta cops don't play that speed racer shit," he replied, walking towards the bar.

"Man fuck these Atlanta cops. I'm out here smoking weed and running lights," Julian stated.

J.R. laughed as his cousin recited a line from their favorite movie *Belly*. Although those words came from DMX, Julian meant every word of it. Like J.R., Julian was in his early twenties, no kids, and very little family with a go-getter attitude that would intimidate the toughest man. He had only been in Atlanta for a few weeks. He hopped on the plane with J.R. after his mother's funeral. He was staying with some chick that lived in Atlanta that he met off Facebook. J.R. offered for him to stay with him but he declined. Julian said *he rather wake up to pussy every morning* in which J.R. definitely understood his reasoning.

"Aye, yo homie here already?" Julian asked once they entered the dimmed bar.

J.R. searched through the small crowed that was there and spotted D'Mani off in the back near the emergency exit. Instead if verbally replying, he pointed in D'Mani's direction and the two headed there.

"Yo Mani, this my cousin Julian. Julian this my bro D'Mani," J.R. said, introducing the strangers.

"What up bro!" the two said unison before J.R. took a seat.

Before they could exchange any other words, a pretty little waitress was at their table, ready to take their orders. Not really hungry, J.R. requested some water while Julian and D'Mani ordered a double shot of Patron. Once the waitress was out of sight, the men got down to business. Both J.R. and D'Mani filled Julian in on what was going on in the streets. It was understood that Julian was stepping in more as an extra man due to Corey being on some other shit. Corey was around more so as the brain of the operations when what they needed was more muscle and that's where Julian stepped in.

"Y'all sound like y'all got some real shit on y'all hands with this Tessa motherfucker," Julian stated, knocking his drink back.

"Nah, not really, to be honest, it's nothing we can't handle," J.R. admitted.

The three men talked and laughed about another twenty minutes before they were ready to leave. Dropping a fifty-dollar tip on the table, they headed out of the door. As soon as they made it to the parking lot, a black Dodge Charger sped past them. The back window rolled down and shots rang out. J.R., D'Mani, and Julian all grabbed their pieces and fired back; one of their bullets flattened the tire of the Dodge Charger, sending it crashing into a wired gate. The three men ran over with their guns still aimed. All three of them having the same thing on their mind. When they made it to the car, the driver was slumped over the sterling wheel while the passenger struggled with the seatbelt. J.R. glanced through the back window where the shots were coming from and found him dead with a gunshot wound to the back of the head.

When the men got a little closer, they realized that the passenger was actually a woman. Other than a few scratches on her head, she looked fine. When she noticed them coming, she tried to reach for her gun, which had fallen under the seat; but with the seatbelt being jammed, she couldn't reach out.

"Aye bitch, you pretty," Julian said, rubbing his pistol on the side of her face.

"FUCK YOU!" she spat.

"Yeah she pretty, but the little bitch rude," J.R. chimed in.

"Who sent you?" D'Mani calmly asked.

"You motherfuckers might as well kill me cause I ain't saying *shit*," she cursed.

"Aight, have it your way," J.R. replied, cocking his gun.

"Nah, that's too easy. Let's get this bitch out. She coming with us," D'Mani stated as he pulled open the jarred door.

The men grabbed the young lady as she kicked and screamed. Patrons from the restaurant as well as other passer-byers started to crowd the streets while sirens could be heard in the distance. They quickly threw her in the trunk of J. R.'s car and sped off. He turned the music up to tune out the sound of her beating on the inside of the trunk and wondered where the fuck he was headed to next.

❧ 18 ❧

The shit with Corey was constantly on Mari's mind. He wanted to kick his own ass for not speaking up when the signs first appeared that something was wrong. Corey wasn't hearing the rehab shit; but the reality was, he was gonna suck it up and go or another bullet was gonna be put in his ass and that shit could come from anybody. With his state of mind, Corey wasn't thinking clearly and everyone had to be their absolute best at all times. They had started a fuckin' war in unknown territory and for anybody to be caught slipping could be detrimental to the entire organization. His ass had already escaped death and D'Mani had even been shot. They still had no fuckin' idea who was behind that, but time would tell. The bitch that D'Mani and Julian had kidnapped still wasn't talking, so they had her hemmed up in the basement. Mari had to give her credit; she was loyal as fuck to whoever sent her, but she would be dead as fuck soon. The plan was to keep her and eventually some pussy niggaz would start looking. Speaking of Mani, his phone rang and it was his twin brother calling.

"What up bruh?" he answered.

"Shit... need a fuckin' backwood and bout ten shots."

"Nigga you still goin' through?"

"Ain't you wit one of the Holiday sisters? Don't act like you don't know how fuckin' stubborn they are."

D'Mari couldn't do shit but laugh because his brother was absolutely right. They loved their women, but it was no secret that they were crazy as hell.

"Point taken... but listen, I been ignoring Drea's comments about that night, so you better fix this shit. Can't believe problems at yo house is affecting my got damn house."

"I'm on it bruh... but did everything work out wit the trucking business? Shit rolling now?"

"Shit is muthafuckin' rolling. I ain't been too long left from meeting wit two of the drivers and shit. This shit finna be like taking candy from a baby." Mari smiled as he thought about how they were about to damn near triple their weekly incomes.

"Aight then... wit this Corey situation? We gon' replace him or what?" Mani inquired.

"I been thinkin' heavy bout that shit. Cuz is just in a fucked up situation right now, but it ain't the end of the road for him. We all deal wit shit differently; he just picked the wrong coping mechanism. I'm headed to get his ass right now to take him to the rehab facility. I think we should bring somebody else in anyway, but not necessarily to take Corey spot. J.R. got a pretty solid partner that'll be a good asset to us," D'Mari explained.

"Yeah, I feel ya. But blood or not, that nigga can't do this kinda shit no mo. It's like we got more got damn problems amongst ourselves than we got wit our enemies. That bitch still ain't talking either, but in time she will."

"Say less... Ima hit you up later after I drop him off. Let me answer Drea's call."

Mari talked to Drea for the rest of the ride to Alyssa and Corey's house. With Thanksgiving and Christmas right around the corner, Drea was in a much better mood. She talked his ear off about how her and her sisters were planning on doing a sleep over and playing different games. D'Mari never put up a fuss because he remembered how Drea told him about sad she was when the Holiday sisters weren't close. Just listening to her plans, Mari knew that he was making the right decision by forcing Corey to get some help. He didn't know how the long the program would last. He had only been instructed that it depended on Corey's level of dependency, but Mari hoped that his cousin would only be gone for a couple of weeks. The hardest part was going to be getting him to stay, but Mari was up for the challenge.

"I'm pulling up now babe. I'll let you know how everything goes... aight... love you too," Mari said and ended the call right after he pulled in behind Alyssa's truck.

D'Mari got out and before he could ring the doorbell, Corey leaned in to dap him up.

"One second bruh... let me take a leak and grab my phone off the charger," Corey told him.

When he rounded the corner, Alyssa appeared and Mari noticed the stressed look on her face. She smiled, but he saw right through it.

"Hey sis... everything gon' be alright. Ima make sure of it," Mari hugged her.

She tried to wipe away the tear that escaped her left eye, but Mari saw it of course.

"Thank you Mari. I know he's gonna put up a fight but let his ass know that if he doesn't get some help... I'm..."

"I got you. Just stay strong and be there for him. He gon' need you," Mari expressed.

Alyssa offered D'Mari something to drink. He grabbed a bottle of water and then Corey emerged from the back.

"I'm ready cuz. Let's go get this money."

"Let's get it," Mari replied.

"I'll see ya later babe. Love ya," Corey kissed his wife.

"I love you too," she gave him a tight hug.

Mari watched the display of affection and knew that he was doing the right thing. Corey bent down and kissed Alyssa's belly and then they dipped out moments later.

They hopped in Mari's car and headed out. He wanted to fire up a blunt, but figured considering the current situation, it would be best to just wait.

"Mani meeting us or you picking him up?" Corey asked as Mari maneuvered into traffic on 285.

"He got some other shit goin' on right now. I'll get up wit his ass later. How you been feeling though?" Mari quizzed, deciding to go ahead and break the ice.

"I'm good bruh. I just had a rough patch, but I swear I'm good. Y'all ain't gotta worry bout me fuckin' up no more. I gotta get myself together for my family."

"And I'm sure you'll do *anything* for your family right? To make sure they straight and shit?"

"Got damn right," Corey replied.

"I figured you would."

Mari kept driving and a few minutes later, he pulled up in front of the rehab facility that he had checked out. Alyssa had already made the arrangements for Corey, but it was setup for him to believe he was checking himself in. If Corey was smart, he would get his shit together without putting up too much of a fuss.

"What the fuck we doing here?" Corey fumed once he finally looked up.

"We here so you can check yourself in and get yo shit together," Mari calmly but firmly replied.

"I just told you I was straight. I don't need this shit," Corey retorted.

"Corey, get out the car, walk inside, check yourself in, and follow whatever treatment plan they give you. This is the *only* option that you'll wanna take."

"You threatening me cuz?"

"You've known me all your life and you know damn well I *don't* make threats. You fucked up some kinda serious. You had members of our fuckin' team *killed* because of yo selfish bullshit. That shit can't be reversed nigga."

"You know what... you right. This bullshit, but Ima do what I gotta do," Corey spat and got out and slammed the door.

D'Mari let that shit slide because he knew that Corey's head was in a fucked up space. He sat there and watched as his cousin walked inside of the doors, and then pulled and headed towards Bankhead so that he could handle some business.

❧ 19 ❧

Corey stood in the entrance of the rehab center and instantly became annoyed. The sight that was before him was an unbearable one. The patients in the center looked like the junkies he'd seen roaming the streets of New York, who was willing to do anything for their next hit. There were a few people admitting their friends or loved ones into the center, and Corey gazed at how the drug or alcohol addict caused a scene as the nurses dragged him down the hall. It reminded him of the scene in New Jack City where Ice-T admitted Chris Rock in a rehab center and how he spazzed out. Seeing a few of the patients in the center and how awful they were made Corey realize that he wasn't in the same the boat as them.

"Fuck this shit!" He walked out of the center, but when he saw that his cousin was still there, Corey paused.

"What the fuck are you doing?" D'Mari yelled from the window.

"Man, this place ain't for me. I'm better off doing this shit at home or something."

"Look nigga, I brought ya ass here so you can learn a

fucking lesson. You may not be strung out, but you *do* have a problem. Maybe with you being away from the people and shit that means the most to you, it'll teach you to *appreciate* what you have. Now take ya ass back inside," his cousin demanded.

Corey was pissed off by the way D'Mari was scolding him, but instead of arguing, he slowly strolled back inside with his hand in his pockets. Once he was back inside, Corey hesitated before making his way to the front desk.

"Good morning and how may I help you?" the middle age Caucasian lady asked with a smile.

"Yeah, uh, my name is Corey Washington and... I want to admit myself in rehab," he spoke in a low tone.

"Okay. Just fill out this paperwork and bring it back when you're finished," she handed him a clip board and pen.

Nodding his head, Corey sat in a nearby seat and examined the form before filling it out. The questions on the forms were simple ones, but when he saw the list of things that people could possibly be addicted to, he was in shock. Corey knew about the basic shit like cocaine, heroin, and Ecstasy; but when he saw shit like cough syrup and bath salt, he couldn't do nothing but shake his head in disbelief. Filling the form out, he checked off all the things that applied to him before returning the form to the receptionist. Corey watched as she read his form for any signs of judgment, but there wasn't one.

"Okay Mr. Washington, I want to start by saying that you made the right decision by admitting yourself into rehab. You might be feeling ashamed or embarrassed that you have to be in a place like this, but just by you being here shows that you want to change your life. Now, once you're in your room, a nurse will come see you and discuss with you how our program works and to get you started with treatment. Here

are few pamphlets that you can read while you wait. Deana
here will escort you to your room."

Corey retrieved the pamphlets then followed the aide to
his room. He peeked inside some on the rooms on the way
down the hall, seeing a few of the patients going through
withdrawal from a lack of drugs. He picked up his pace a
little bit as they neared the end of the hallway.

"A nurse will be in shortly to see you," the beautiful young
black woman spoke.

"Cool."

"Do you need anything?"

"Nah, I'm straight."

"Okay. Well just let me know if you do," Deana smiled,
closing the door behind her.

Corey scanned the room and a feeling of depression
quickly came over him as he examined the plain white walls.
He sat down on the twin size bed, placing the pamphlets on
the wooden nightstand. The blinds on the window were open
and he gazed out of it. Corey never thought that he would
ever be in a rehabilitation; but then again, he never thought
that he would become addicted to pills, alcohol, and gambling
either. Corey analyzed the last few months of his life and how
a night of gambling had turned his world upside down. He
went from being on a winning streak to losing almost everything. When his winning streak was over, Corey was certain
that he'd win it back but ended up losing all of his winnings
and damn near the shirt he was wearing. After being thrown
out, Lou gave him deadline for him to have the money that he
owed him. That was the night that changed his life forever.

As Corey continued to stare out the window, he started to
regret letting his ex co-worker convince him to go gambling
with him; but he couldn't deny the fact that he enjoyed the
thrill of winning, but he let gambling destroy him. Although

he was embarrassed to be there with people that were worse off than he was, a small part of Corey was cool with him being there. Since he was free from all the lies and secrets, he needed to be free from the pills and alcohol that he often craved.

A few moments later, a nurse came into his room and they discussed the severity of his problem. After spending over an hour discussing his issues, the nurse informed him that he would began detoxing the next day. She explained the withdrawal symptoms that he would be going through, and Corey admitted that he'd been feeling depressed and having anger fits for the past couple of days. Instead of waiting until the next the day to start his detox, the nurse decided that it would be best he started right away. When the nurse left out the room, Corey pulled out his phone and found the ultra sound pictures his wife sent him. He smiled before scrolling to a picture of his wife exposing her baby bump.

"You don't know how bad I wanna leave this place Lyssa, but I promised you that I would come and get clean. I'm doing this for us, baby. I love y'all."

Corey hated being away from his family and his biggest fear was something happening to Alyssa while he was in there. He knew that his family would take care of her but that wasn't their job. It was his. Instead of filling his head with negative thoughts, Corey thought about what him being there meant and what the outcome was going to be. He needed for this time to fly by quickly, so he could be back with his family and back running the business.

20

D'Mani sat up in bed and looked at his surroundings dejectedly. It wasn't that there was anything really wrong with the room. It was just that he would have rather been waking up in his own plush bed next to his woman, but that shit wasn't gone happen. A week had passed since D'Mari had come and gotten him from Cheyanne's in the middle of the night. Turned out that the reason Anastasia hadn't followed him out the house was because she had the *find my iPhone* app on his phone. She'd known exactly where he was at the whole time. His brother told him that he only got hip to the situation when his wife tried to sneak out of the house dressed like a damn ninja. D'Mani couldn't lie; he was glad that Mari was able to intercept the bullshit because if Stasia and her sisters had been the ones knocking, then it would have been a whole other set of problems. The sisters would have definitely come and whooped ass first, then asked questions later, and he didn't want Cheyanne in a scuffle over a misunderstanding.

Instead of going home and dealing with his girl's attitude, he had his brother take him to their mama's house, all the while ignoring Stasia's numerous calls and texts that were coming through back to back. His brother talked shit the whole way but that shit was going in one ear and out the other. Mani hadn't done anything wrong, but it seemed like everybody was ready to blame him without even getting his side of the story. And when they'd pulled up to their ma's crib, she was no different. Snapping on him about not meeting her grand baby and all types of shit. She didn't even care about the fact that his leg was fucked up. By the time she was done with him, D'Mari had took his ass back home and it was nearing three in the morning, but the texts were still coming from Anastasia. They just went from bad to worse and the last one let him know that he wasn't welcome in their crib.

On one hand, Mani felt like he should fight her on that, mainly because it was her own paranoia and insecurities that were putting a wedge between them; but on the other, he figured that maybe they *did* need a break from each other. Things had definitely been hectic for them since Cheyanne and Imani stepped on the scene, and the way she'd been acting had him really not feeling her. It was a week later and things hadn't gotten any better. He was just fed up with the whole situation.

"Why you still sittin' in bed like you ain't just hear me callin' you?" his mother's voice interrupted the thoughts he had swimming around in his head. He looked up to see her small frame standing in the doorway with her hands on her hips.

"My bad ma, I was thinkin'," he told her with a sigh. Her face briefly showed concern before turning hard again.

"Oh you must be thinkin' bout bringin' my grand diva over here to finally meet me?" she huffed, shifting her weight to one leg. He started to tell her ass that, that was the exact *opposite* of what he'd been thinking; but in all honesty, he did need to go and see his little princess. D'Mani hadn't been back to Cheyanne's since the bullshit the week before, in an attempt to not make the situation worse; but he knew he couldn't do that forever.

"Yeah lemme call her mama up and see if I can come through."

"Ain't you *"comin' through"* what got yo ass in my guestroom now?" she questioned.

"Hell-" D'Mani paused briefly when she glared at him for cursing. "I mean naw man... Anastasia is what got me here, but I do need to go get lil mama and Ky," he admitted.

"Well good luck with getting Kyler cause Anastasia just dropped all your clothes off on the curb, so I doubt if she want yo ass goin' over there." Her voice was sugary sweet, but D'Mani knew she was being smart. He hopped up from his spot on the bed and ran over to the window that faced the front yard to see that she was right. There was about five garbage bags and three suitcases sitting out front exactly where his mother said they were. For Anastasia to have packed all of the clothes he had at home, she would have to have been up all night with all her damn sisters over there helping.

"You ain't try to stop her ma... man what the fuck?!" he turned away from the window to address her and ran right into an open hand smack.

Whap!

"Boy don't get yo ass beat in here! You ain't that damn mad. Besides why the fuck would I try and stop her? You should have took yo ass home last week," she huffed, swatting at him again.

"Ayite, my bad ma-"

"Yeah, yo bad! Go bring that shit in here and come eat," she snapped, hitting him with an eye roll before leaving the room.

D'Mani hurried up and got the fuck out of there. He really hadn't meant to curse at her because no matter what, he loved and respected his O.G. She had taken the best care she could of him and his brother after their father died in a drug deal gone bad. Though she'd never really told them much about the man, she had made it clear that she didn't want the same life for them; but the hustle was obviously in their blood. The call of the streets had them ditching school and moving packs as early as age fifteen. They managed to hide it from her up until their senior year, but once they moved up in rank, there was no keeping the shit a secret. Of course, she wasn't happy about it. In fact, she had stopped speaking to them both, but it didn't even take six months before she relented. As a mother, she couldn't let a petty disagreement stop her from seeing her boys, but they knew that she worried about them. That had always been evident. When they made the move south, it didn't take much convincing at all for her to get on board with moving. The house was spacious as hell and D'Mani was thankful because it was looking like he might be there for longer than he had planned.

After making what felt like twenty trips to bring all of his shit in, Mani went to the kitchen where his mother was sitting at the table drinking a cup of coffee. She motioned to the chair across from her at a plate piled high with cheese eggs, bacon, grits and biscuits, and he didn't hesitate to take a seat. D'Mani couldn't say that his girl didn't try, but she wasn't very talented in the kitchen, so it had been a long time since he'd eaten some real good food. He sat down and immediately began to scarf down the breakfast while his mama sat across from him silently drinking her coffee.

"You know," she started and he went still, knowing she was about to say something crazy. "I kinda like this Anastasia girl, she doesn't seem like a pushover. If it was me, I woulda cut you," she shrugged like what she had said was normal.

"Man, I ain't go over there on no bull- on nothin'. I was just tryna get some sleep, but I left my wallet, so I went to the closest spot I could."

She didn't say anything right away. She just sat there blinking at him with her nose turned up.

"That shit sound stupid. I would've put yo ass out too." She rolled her eyes for what seemed like the hundredth time and moved to put her mug in the sink. "Well either way, I believe you, so I'm gonna help you get back home cause I can't have you over here cock blocking," she said, making D'Mani choke on the eggs he'd just stuffed into his mouth.

"What you mean cock blockin'? You bet not ne havin' no old niggas comin' through here," he managed to get out between coughs.

"I mean exactly what I said, and why he gotta be old? I like my men young hmph," she tittered with a neck roll.

"Yep, that's it! I'm up!" D'Mani jumped up from the table with only half his food gone, but he wasn't tryna sit and hear her talking about what she did and didn't like in men. He dumped the plate and sat it in the sink, knowing that his mama didn't like other people washing her dishes.

"Wait! I'm supposed to be helpin' you get yo girl back!" she yelled as he exited the kitchen.

"When I get back!" he tossed over his shoulder without stopping. There was still work to do at the traps, and he'd much rather do that than sit there with her ass. He showered quickly and found some light gray joggers and a black Nike shirt to throw on. A part of him was surprised that Stasia hadn't put bleach on his shit; but then again, she wasn't the type to do some shit like that, despite how she'd been acting recently.

Once he was behind the wheel of his car, D'Mani tried to

ring her phone, but it went straight to voicemail. He figured she had blocked him. After he took care of his business and brought Imani to see his mother, he'd try to call again; and if that ain't work, he'd pop up over there. Stasia wasn't about to cut him out her life completely over a misunderstanding. There was *no way* he was gone let that happen no matter what she thought she was doing.

❧ 21 ❧

J.R. grabbed the Wal-Mart bags out of the trunk and headed in the house. He and Lexi had been out shopping all day. They started the morning off by grabbing breakfast at the Waffle House. They stuffed their faces, reminiscing about how they met two years prior at the same spot. At the time, Lexi was a stripper, and although J.R. hated those type of bitches, it was something about her that drew him in. After eating, they headed to the mall where they picked up a gang of shit. J.R. made Lexi put down everything that she picked up for the baby. Although she was five months and it was ok to start shopping, neither of them had any idea on what they were having, so he made her wait it out. They started decorating the baby room with neutral colors but that was about it.

"DAMN, YOU NOT GON' GET ONE BAG ALEXIS?" J.R. ASKED, slamming the trunk closed with his hands full of bags.

"I GOT A BAG HOMIE," SHE REPLIED, HOLDING HER FOOD from *Wendy's* high in the air.

J.R. SHOOK HIS HEAD AND PROCEEDED TOWARDS THE HOUSE. He waited on Lexi to walk onto the porch and used her key. After digging in the bag and eating a few fries, she finally got her keys out of her purse and allowed them access into their home.

When the couple walked in, they were shocked to see two females and four guys sitting in their living room, drinking and playing cards. J.R. felt his blood boiling instantly. He looked over at Lexi, who he knew was ready to pop off too.

J.R. dropped all the bags on the floor, pulled his pistol from his waist, and joined the gang. Yasmine noticed him coming first, and she quickly jumped up from the boy's lap she was sitting on; but it was too late, the damage was already done.

"YOU LIL UGLY MOTHERFUCKERS GOT THIRTY SECONDS TO get the fuck out of my house," he yelled, cocking his gun.

THE YOUNG BOYS' EYES GREW THE SIZE OF GOLF BALLS AS they scattered like roaches when you cut the kitchen light on. Once the living room was clear, J.R. turned the music down and focused on Yasmine, who looked like she wanted to run out as well.

"YOU MUST BE OUT YO MOTHERFUCKIN' MIND... HAVING these niggas in my house," Lexi snapped first, walking towards Yasmine.

"IF I'M NOT MISTAKING, THIS MY BROTHER HOUSE," SHE snapped back, rolling her eyes and neck.

"LIL GIRL, I WILL BEAT THE DOG SHIT OUT OF YOU," LEXI yelled, pulling off her jean jacket, ready to attack.

"Y'ALL NEED TO CALM THE FUCK DOWN. FIRST AND foremost, if I EVER hear you disrespecting my girl, I'll slap the shit outta you myself."

"BUT JEREMY…"

"SHUT THE FUCK UP! I AIN'T TRYING TO HEAR NOTHING YOU have to say, but you heard what the fuck I said. It's TWO grown motherfuckers in this house and *you* not one of them. Moving forward, you can't *shit* in my crib without asking permission first. Now get the fuck out my face," he barked.

YASMINE DIDN'T BOTHER TO OPEN HER MOUTH; INSTEAD, she did as instructed.

"NAH, AS A MATTER OF FACT. CLEAN THIS SHIT UP AND then get the fuck out my face," he demanded.

J.R. LEFT YASMINE ALONG WITH HER MESS AND HEADED UP

the stairs with Lexi in tow. When they reached their bedroom, he slammed the door, went inside the nightstand for his weed stash, and started rolling up. To say he was pissed would be an understatement. He didn't have a problem with Yas making friends, seeing how Atlanta was her new home; but she went about it wrong. J.R. did too much shit in the streets to be having random niggas and bitches in his spot. He knew Yasmine only knew so much, but she still knew better; and if she didn't, she did now.

After rolling the blunt, J.R. lit it and walked out the door, without saying another word to anyone else. He hopped in the car and drove with no destination in mind. Making it to the city, his phone began to ring off the hook. He has ignored the first five calls but decided to answer when D'Mari called again.

"WHAT UP BRUH?" HE ASKED DRYLY.

"MAKE YO WAY TO THE TRAP IN ZONE 6.... ASAP!" MARI barked before abruptly ending the call.

J.R. BUSTED A U-TURN IN THE MIDDLE OF THE STREET. HE had just passed that particular trap house a few blocks back. He should have gone with his first mind because something told him to stop through there when he drove past. Arriving about two minutes later, J.R. was running up the stairs, ready to check things out. As soon as he entered the home, the smell of old blood filled his nostrils and he knew something was wrong. Walking further in the house, he noticed a body in the kitchen and two others laid with a gunshot wounds to the head in the hallway. A fourth body was found in the bathroom while the last person laid in a puddle of blood in one of the bedrooms.

"WHAT THE FUCK?" HE CURSED TO HIMSELF WHILE HE looked around.

"THIS SHIT CRAZY," MARI SAID, WALKING INTO THE bedroom with D'Mani and Julian behind him.

"SO THIS HOW NIGGAS DO IN ATLANTA HUH?" JULIAN smirked, amazed at the sight before him.

"I WONDER WHO DID THIS SHIT?" MARI QUIZZED.
J.R. turned around and the word that was written in blood on the wall let him know that they didn't have too far to look.

🌿 2 2 🌿

"We need to talk Mari," he heard his wife say as he was straightening his tie.

"Yeah babe... what's up?"

"You ready to tell me bout the shit you into yet?" Drea quizzed.

"Nope," he walked over and kissed her on the lips and then grabbed his phone and keys and dipped out.

"D'Mari Mitchell... you better..."

"Just trust me baby... just *trust* me. I love you," he called out to her and headed down the hall.

Mari made a pit stop at the twins' room and looked in on them. It was only a little after seven and they both were still sleeping. After kissing both of them on the forehead, he dipped out before Drea could continue on with her investigation. The lawyer part of her mixed with the nosiness could be lethal at times. She had been asking D'Mari twenty-one questions every single day, but he was true to his word. The less she knew the better. He had no intentions on involving her in any of his illegal shit. Mari had a few stops on his agenda for the day and he could just smell the money that was being made.

Two hours later, Mari had met with yet another investor and felt confident as hell that his team would be able to retire within five years tops because of the decisions they were making. They were being shot at it seemed like every fuckin' day and that alone made him invest more of their money into legal shit so that none of their wives would have to bury their asses. He was set to show Julian some more of the ropes in a couple of hours, but family came first. Mari parked at the rehab facility and got out so that he could check on his cousin. It still didn't sit well with him that innocent soldiers had been killed behind Corey's lies, but what's done was done.

"Well hello handsome. What can I do to you... I mean for you?" the receptionist boldly flirted.

"Hi, I'm here to visit with Corey Washington," Mari replied, keeping it cordial.

"Visitation starts in ten minutes. You can sign in and I'll keep you company while you wait."

"I'm good luv, enjoy," Mari replied while he signed in.

"D'Mari Mitchell. I always liked the last name Mitchell. Watch me make it happen," Janice replied.

Mari went and sat down and ignored everything that Janice was saying. He looked up the stats on recent stocks that he invested in to pass time. A couple other people walked in for visitation and that was his cue to get up. He bypassed Janice and went to the back. After talking to Corey the night before, he already knew where to go. He spotted his cousin as soon as he rounded the corner and they dapped each other up.

"How's it goin' man?" Mari quizzed.

"Shit, best as can be I guess. I'm just doin' what I gotta do to get my family back and get my spot back in the empire," Corey admitted.

"Just do what you gotta do man... we gon' hold it down for ya. We added one of J.R.'s cousins just to get some extra manpower."

"So y'all niggaz done replaced me already?"

"Nigga, don't look at it like that. You did make a couple of our top soldiers disappear, remember?" Mari reminded him and Corey's demeanor instantly went back to normal.

"My bad... this just a fucked up situation. Y'all don't feel me though."

"If we didn't feel you, yo ass would be six feet under, but let's not forget this shit is a result to what you did... but let's change the subject to something calmer. How they treating you in here?"

"It's straight. I got a group meeting in a few. I really been to myself, but I guess I gotta get acquainted wit some of these other mofos in here. I ain't gon' lie, being in here done made me not wanna take shit else or drink shit else. I thought my problems was bad, but these niggaz done did shit worse than me," Corey confessed.

D'Mari and Corey chopped it up for about fifteen more minutes and then the visitation for that hour was over. Alyssa was visiting him later and Mari was happy. He knew that Corey needed to know that everybody still had his back. He walked back out front and bumped straight into Janice. It seemed as if she was waiting on him.

"I can be *Andrea* if you want me to be," she whispered.

"What the fuck?" Mari stopped dead in his tracks.

Instead of replying, Janice took off and exited into a door that was locked when he turned the knob. He wondered how in the fuck she knew Drea or was it just a coincidence. He hoped it was the latter, but it would be a lie if he said the shit didn't bother him.

"Yo, have lil homie meet me at the spot in Bankhead," Mari told J.R. as soon as he answered the phone.

"Bet," J.R. responded and hung up.

Mari made one stop by *Wendy's* and grabbed a 4-4-4 and a spicy chicken meal. He smashed his chicken sandwich and fries and guzzled down the last of his bottled water right as he pulled up to the spot. A black Challenger was sitting in the driveway, so he knew that it had to be Julian because no one else should have been there. Mari got out and noticed Julian getting out at the same time.

"If you ain't early, you late," Julian used Mari's line against him since he knew that it was his number one rule.

"I had to get the bitch some food," Mari held up the bag and smirked.

Even though he wasn't late, he had mad respect that Julian was paying attention to what was being said. They made their way around back, went inside, and then headed down to the basement.

"Here, Ima watch you work today," he handed Julian the bag.

"Word?" Julian smiled hard as hell like he had just won the lottery.

Mari didn't know what he had in mind, but he had a front row seat and was ready to witness it.

✢ 23 ✢

Corey sat in the last row listening to the scandalous shit the residents did for drugs in his weekly so-called bonding session with the shrink. He sat with his arms folded the entire time with his eyes closed shaking his head at the stories that were being told. One chick traded her five year old for a hit while a man let the drug dealers rape his wife for his next high. Corey wanted to tell all those motherfuckers how sick and twisted they were but the conversation he had earlier with his cousin quickly humbled him. He may not have given his family up for drugs but putting them in harm's way behind his bullshit was just as bad.

Corey briefly tuned into the conversation for a few minutes then tuned them back out when a man began to cry about what he lost and how he was ready to leave. The thought of his brothers bringing in extra help to fill his spot low key bothered him. He knew his cousin disregarded the fact that he wasn't being replaced but he felt like that was D'Mari's way of keeping him calm and down playing the situation. The thought of a nigga taking his spot, regardless of who it was didn't sit right with Corey at all but, instead of being bitter about it, it just made him want to work harder to get the fuck out of there.

"Mr. Washington,"

"What?" he didn't hide his annoyance.

"Would you like to share with us this week?" Dr. Fields, the psychologist, questioned.

"Nah. I'm straight," he sighed.

"Okay but need I remind you that the more you refuse to participate, the longer you'll have to stay in here. They'll assume that you're not willing to face your problems and kick your addiction fully."

Corey shot her a glare that let her know that he clearly didn't give a fuck and to stop talking to him.

"How about you sir?" She pointed to the nigga in the row in front of him a few seats over to the left.

"I don't wanna share my business with these pathetic motherfuckers in here. The fuck I look like? "He spat.

"You don't have to be rude. Everyone in here is trying to kick their habits and get their lives back on track. In one way or another, all of you are in the same boat. So, there's no need for name calling or judgement. With that being said, I want to thank all that participated this week and we'll meet again next week. Same time. Same room," she dismissed the meeting with a smile.

"About fucking time," Corey stood up to leave heading back to his room.

"There's my handsome husband," the sound of Alyssa's soft voice caught his attention.

The sight of his wife waddling down the hall in her red and black Victoria Secret Pink sweat suit and red retro Jordan 12's put a smile on his face.

"Hey baby. I thought I missed you. Our meeting ran longer than expected," he embraced her.

"Well I guess that's a good thing. I thought I was gonna be late. There was a slight pain in my stomach and I thought I was gonna have to go to the hospital but it went away as quickly as it came."

"I don't like the sound of that. Is this the first time you felt this pain?" he asked with concern.

"Yes, Corey."

"Alyssa?"

"It happened twice and the pain doesn't last that long. Its's nothing to worry about," she walked past him and took a seat in his room.

"We talk everyday Alyssa why am I just now hearing about this? Corey sat down beside her.

"I know I shoulda told you, but you got enough on your mind and I need you to focus on getting out of here. If something happens, my sisters can take care of me."

"I don't give a fuck about none of that. You're my wife and I wanna know everything that's going on with you. You hear me?"

Alyssa nodded her head as she glanced down at the floor. Corey noticed how Alyssa seemed to be keeping something from him at that moment and needed to address it.

"What's on your mind bae?"

"Corey, I know we haven't talked much about you lying to me about your job, you being in the hospital or what the hell you've gotten yourself involved in that caused you to be in here and I know you don't wanna talk about it but can I ask a question?"

"Yeah," afraid of the question.

"What started all of this? The drinking, the pill popping and the constant lying?"

"It was my way of dealing with losing my job. I knew you would be upset and I didn't want you to stress about how shit

126

was going to get paid or make you feel like you had to pick up my slack," he partially lied.

"Baby, you know if you would've told me what was going on, we could've handled this shit together. You started drinking your life away and popping pills and shit. I'm not trying to be insensitive or anything but all this shit could've been avoided if you would've opened your mouth bae," Alyssa rolled her eyes.

"So, I've been told," he mumbled.

Despite the guilt he felt about lying to his wife yet again, the rest of their visit went well spending most of their time talking about the baby and feeling her kick. When the visit came to an end, Corey kissed his wife goodbye before watching her walk out the facility doors and wishing he was going with her.

"How far along is she?" a man stood beside him.

"What?"

"Your wife. How far along is she?"

"How do you know that's my wife?"

"By the way your staring at her, making sure she's cool as she walks to her car and the band on your finger. Niggas don't wait around for a female to be out sight before they move if she ain't important."

Corey nodded in agreement.

"She'll be eight months soon."

"Boy or girl?"

"Girl," Corey smirked keeping his eyes on Alyssa as she pulled off in her car.

"That's wassup," he nodded.

"Weren't you in the meeting earlier?" Corey finally paid attention to the nigga that was talking to him.

"Yeah. I usually keep to myself but you seem like the only normal motherfucka in here. So, I figured I'd try to something different and be the fuck friendly," he chuckled. "Larry," he extended his hand.

"Corey."

Although he wasn't trying to make friends with the whackos in the facility, he felt like Larry was a cool a dude was more like him than the junkies they both steered clear from. Corey didn't have any reason to be suspicious of his new acquaintance but the way his brothers trained him and what he had proven to himself was that you can't trust everybody. Learning from the mistakes he made, he decided to be on his toes at all and start being mindful of the company he kept.

24

"Aye boss man, we got a problem over here in Bankhead." A worker named Twan said as soon as D'Mani answered his phone. The word problem immediately put him on high alert, since him and his team had been dealing with so much shit as of late. D'Mani looked over at Kyler and Imani and instantly felt bad about having to cut their day short. He had already not been able to spend a lot of time with Kyler, because of Anastasia's bullshit, and now when he'd finally gotten the two kids together he was going to have to leave them.

"Say less, I'ma be there in a minute." D'Mani told him and hung up. Across the table Kyler and Imani weren't paying him any attention. She was busy telling Kyler about her birthday party that would be coming up in December, and he was pretty much eating out of the palm of her hand. D'Mani loved how good the two got along, he just wished that Kyler's mama was as open to the situation as he was. "hey yall, I'm gone have to take you home so I can go handle something real quick."

"Awww man! Do we gotta go?" Kyler asked.

"Yeah, do we gotta go?" Imani pouted.

D'Mani realized that he had to be strong, cause the puppy dog face she was giving him, had him ready to say fuck the trap out in Bankhead. Catching on to what she was doing Kyler also put on the saddest face he could muster, hoping to get D'Mani to change his mind.

"Yeah, we gotta go, but I promise that I'll make it up to yall ok. Maybe we can go see a movie or something next week." He offered with a smile and they both seemed to be satisfied, for the moment.

"Ayite, but we gone need big snacks, ain't that right Mani?" Kyler asked and she nodded firmly.

"Yep! Big snacks!" Imani agreed.

"Ayite yall got that," D'Mani told them, relieved that the issue had blown over and they were both satisfied. The two cheered happily and D'Mani helped them to clear the table, before they all filed out of McDonald's and to his truck. He figured he would call Stasia first since she lived closer to where he was, but the phone kept going straight to voicemail.

After trying to call her three times he gave up realizing that she had probably cut her phone off on some petty shit. She had mentioned that she was going to get her hair done though so he knew she wasn't home and he wasn't bout to go through his list of contacts to find somebody to get the kids while he dealt whatever was going on at the trap. Hoping that it wouldn't be too much of an issue, D'Mani headed to Cheyanne's house. She was off since it was the weekend, and had planned on sitting around the house. He said a silent prayer that, that hadn't changed as he pulled up. D'Mani breathed a sigh of relief when he saw her car still sitting in the same spot it had been when he'd left there an hour before.

"Come on yall." He said taking the keys out. Kyler looked at him funny, but didn't say anything as he followed Imani out of the car and up to the front door. It didn't take long for Cheyanne to answer the door, dressed in some black leggings, and a white tank top that had her cleavage on full display. D'Mani couldn't help but take in how shapely she was as his eyes traveled the length of her, stopping at her exposed chest. Cheyanne cleared her throat to get his attention and raised a questioning brow, while Imani gave her a quick hey and ran inside.

"Is everything okay?" she wanted to know.

"My bad, umm yeah." D'Mani stuttered as he tried to get his head back in the right place. "I got a work emergency so I gotta cut today short, but Stasia ain't answering her phone, I can't get ahold of nobody else and I'm really pressed for time so I was wondering...." His voice trailed off as he tried to will himself to ask her to keep Kyler for him.

"Oh, yeah sure, I'll keep an eye on him." She nodded with a shrug, catching on to what D'Mani was trying to ask. Relief flooded him. He hadn't really known what to expect when he decided to come there, but he was glad that Cheyanne was willing to take Kyler in. He couldn't help but wonder though if it would have been as easy to get Stasia to do the same thing with Imani. Turning to Kyler he noted the confused look on the boys face and placed a hand on his shoulder.

"Aye man, I need you to stay over here with Cheyanne and Mani for a lil bit, until I get back ayite?" he told him. Kyler looked between him and Cheyanne like he didn't know if staying there was a good idea or not, but at that point he didn't have a choice. D'Mani had already wasted too much time as it was. Seeing that he was struggling, Cheyanne stooped down in front of Kyler and gave him a reassuring smile.

"Hey, I'm Cheyanne." She said sticking her hand out for him to shake. Which surprisingly, he did. "It's okay if you come in for awhile, I swear I don't bite." She joked holding up the scout fingers.

"I bite!" Imani shouted out the door. D'Mani and Cheyanne laughed as she stood to her feet.

"Imani ain't nobody biting!" Cheyanne said rolling her eyes. "Come on Ky." He looked to D'Mani for reassurance, and once he nodded for him to go Kyler stepped forward into the house and then ran off to play with Imani.

"Okay, he's good for now, just don't be tryna be gone for no long ass time, cause I'm not tryna deal with his mama." She warned.

"Thanks man, I owe you, and I'ma be back soon, this should only take an hour maybe two." D'Mani said stepping down the porch.

"Mmm Hmm."

He knew that she was going to hold him to that shit, but she didn't understand how much he appreciated her doing him that solid. As much as he didn't want to he was beginning to see Cheyanne as more than just someone to coparent with. The way that Stasia had been acting was pushing him away and the way Cheyanne was coming was actually pulling him in. D'Mani didn't want to lose his woman though. He loved Anastasia, but was finding it harder and harder to deal with her bullshit. D'Mani pushed thoughts of Cheyanne and his issues with Anastasia to the back of his mind as he pulled away. He didn't need to be distracted while he handled business, but once he was done he planned on finding Stasia so that they could work out their problems, before he was tempted to do something stupid.

Exactly an hour and a half later D'Mani had diffused the situation at the trap, which wasn't really too big of a deal and was headed back to take Kyler back to his mama. His phone vibrated on his leg letting him know that he still hadn't checked his messages since leaving but he was in a rush. To him the less time that Kyler spent over at Cheyanne's the better, because if Stasia found out there was no telling how ignorant she'd get.

When he pulled up to Stasia's house her car was out front letting him know that she had finally brought her ass back home. Him and Kyler climbed out and made their way up the stairs. The door flew open and she stood there like looking at D'Mani angrily.

"Why didn't you answer my calls?" she asked rolling her neck so that her freshly done hair moved fluidly. D'Mani was poised to compliment how good she looked and have an adult conversation with her about the course of their relationship, but she killed that the moment she opened her mouth.

"My phone was on silent." He shrugged all of a sudden not wanting to talk too much at that point. Turning to Kyler he rubbed the top of his head. "I'ma see you later lil man."

D'Mani didn't even wait for a response as he hurried to get back into his car and pull away ready to go back to his mama's crib and get some much needed sleep. Things with Anastasia had taken a crazy turn and he just wasn't sure where they would be going after this, if there was anywhere to go with the relationship. With their future heavy on his mind D'Mani answered his vibrating phone without paying any attention to who the caller was.

"Wassup."

"I know yo ugly ass did NOT take my baby to that bitch house D'Mani!" Anastasia barked into his ear and continued before he could even say anything. "You really showin the fuck out right now for real, but if you think that I'm bouta play this lil baby mama game with you, you really got me fucked up! Don't even THINK about bringing your ass over here for my son nigga! That shit all the way dead!" and then the line went silent so he knew that she had hung up. Instead of going with his first mind and going back to her house to put her ass in her place D'Mani continued on his route. He wasn't sure how things would go if he went back there and the last thing he wanted was to end up putting his hands on Stasia or argue with her while Kyler was around. For the time being, he would grant her wish and leave her the fuck alone, and in turn leave Kyler alone too. It really hurt him to have to stop fucking with Kyler for the moment, but things with Stasia were turning volatile if he was thinking about putting hands on her. He just hoped that at some point she realized that she was ruining them and got her shit together before she lost him forever.

25

It was the day before Thanksgiving which was usually J.R.'s favorite holiday but with his mom gone, he wasn't is the mood. He knew with Christmas being right around the corner, he was going to be missing her even more. J.R. beat himself up because last year, he spent the holidays with Lexi and her family, he had no idea that he would never spend another holiday with his mom. Even worst, he didn't know how Yasmine would take things. Since snapping on her about the company she had in his house, tension had been high amongst the siblings. She was always in her room. She walked around with her face frowned up. Even her and Lexi exchanged a few words here and there. J.R. knew Yasmine was dealing with shit bigger than her but she needed to understand that it's life.

"Here she come right now." Lexi said, snapping J.R. out of his thoughts.

He looked up and spotted Lexi's auntie Shirley, walking through the airport doors. Both J.R. and Lexi laughed, she came through strutting in a pink and green floral sweater, a yellow fanny pack and a pair of blue leggings.

"This lady look a mess." Lexi gushed as J.R. got out the car to help with her bags.

J.R. had never met a person on Earth like Aunt Shirley. She was a piece of work but either you loved her or hated her, there was no gray areas. J.R. met her halfway, snatching up her bags and placing them in the backseat. As soon as she seen him, she smiled and licked her lips. J.R. laughed to himself as he prepared for the hour drive back to their house.

"Aunttttiiiiieeeee what up bitch!" Lexi smiled, turning around in her seat once the backdoor closed.

"My favorite niece, what's up. I missed you. Damn, yo nose sitting across yo face. Lil Shirley making you ugly." She frowned.

"Who the fuck is Lil Shirley?" J.R. turned around and asked.

"You know what, you right. Maybe we shouldn't name the baby after me, seeing how I'm ya mistress and whatnot." She replied, reaching forward, massaging J.R.'s shoulders.

"Girl, if you don't get yo hands of my man...."

"OUR man." Shirley corrected her, sitting back and getting comfortable.

J.R. laughed as they argued the rest of the ride. Lexi and Shirley gossiped about the rest of the family. He couldn't believe how messy the two was.

"You know I'm mad you pregnant. Who I'm supposed to smoke with now?" she whined.

"Auntie, I'm sorry. How selfish of me." She giggled, nudging J.R. with her elbow.

"You know a little weed not gon hurt right?" she urged.

"Auntie, she aint smoking but I got a blunt with ya name on it as soon as we pull up." J.R. advised her.

"I knew you wanted me as much as I wanted you." She stated, cheesing from ear to ear.

After arguing with his girl's aunt for another twenty

minutes, they pulled up to D'Mari and Andrea's house. As soon as J.R. stopped the car, Aunt Shirley began to fuss.

"Hell naw. No. Hell no. I'm not staying here." She snapped.

"I told yo ass if I wasn't staying at yall place then I wasn't coming. J.R. take me back to Mississippi cuz this some bull-shit." She continued.

"Girl shut up. We only visiting." Lexi replied, getting out the car.

"Aw. Somebody better tell me something cuz......"

"Auntie just get out the car and come on.... DAMN!" J.R. yelled getting frustrated with the entire situation.

He was happy to see that D'Mari's car was in the driveway. There was no way in hell he was going to be able to deal with the Holiday sisters alone.

"That's what I'm talking about baby. Put me in my place." Aunt Shirley gloated, finally catching up to them on the porch.

Lexi used her key to gain access to her sister's house. When they walked in, everyone was sitting in the living room, laughing about something. Lexi's mom Victoria arrived in Atlanta the night before.

J.R. could smell food cooking from the kitchen, which made his stomach growl. He wanted to roll a blunt, eat, shit and then take a nap. After speaking to everyone and getting acquainted. J.R. and D'Mari dipped off to his man cave and rapped about things from there.

"So, is the bitch in the basement talking yet?" D'Mari asked, opening up a bottle of water he grabbed from his mini-ridge.

"Hell nah, the bitch stubborn as fuck. She won't really eat shit. She gon fuck around and kill herself." J.R. replied, grabbing and unlocking his phone.

"Cool with me, it aint like she gon make it out alive anyway. Have you talked to Corey?" Mari quizzed.

"Nah, I gotta go see my mans once the holidays over. How he holding up?"

"He good. I like the work Julian putting in."

"I told you. We got the same blood flowing through our veins. We a rare breed." J.R. boosted.

The two of them talked about everything from drugs to women. J.R. had to admit, although he hadn't known them long, they always came through and had his back. Taking over was taking longer than expected due to the war in the streets but once they handled that, they'll be rich and it'll all be worth it.

D'Mani arrived and joined them in the basement, adding his drama into their conversation mix. J.R. always thought Lexi was the feisty sister but hearing all the shit about Anastasia, he changed his mind quickly.

J.R. listened on attentively until his phone vibrated. He prayed it wasn't some more bullshit regarding their trap houses. He was relieved to see that it was actually Yasmine calling instead. Snatching the phone off of the couch, he answered before she could hang up.

"Yeah...."

"Hey bruh, I have a question. I was going through mom's box and came across some shit." Yasmine stated.

"Ok Yas, what is it?" he asked, trying to get to the point.

"Well, you know my birth certificate was in there, along with mommies and yours but yours looked funny." She replied.

"Funny how?" he quizzed.

"Pops name not on yours, it's some nigga name Justin Tessa...... who is that?"

❧ 26 ❧

It seemed like Thanksgiving had just passed, but there it was again. The biggest difference, it was the first Thanksgiving in Atlanta and everyone was having a good ass time. If someone would have told D'Mari one year ago that he would be married with kids, and not living in New York, he would have called them a got damn lie. But, there he was. The night before had been very eventful and Mari expected nothing less for the main day. With the business that they were in, no one was ever technically 'off', but they were somewhat off so that they could enjoy the family. After hopping out of the shower and drying off, Mari got dressed in a pair of grey joggers and a New York Giants tee shirt. He had been a Giants fan for as long as he could remember and would always bet on them even when they had a shitty ass team. His team was playing the Cowboys later that evening and one of the younger workers had placed a five thousand dollar bet with him. Deep down, Mari felt like he was about to donate some money to the youngster, but he would never admit the shit.

When Mari glanced at the clock on the nightstand, it was

forty minutes after ten and they were scheduled to eat at noon. He made his way to the living room where he found his mother in law, Victoria feeding DJ some mashed potatoes. Drea fussed with her the night before about giving the babies table food, but Victoria said she started feeding all of her children from the table when they were five months so that meant the twins were one month behind in her eyes. Drea finally decided to throw in the towel because she was fighting a losing battle. His mom, Linda, and Aunt Shirley agreed so D'Mari stayed out of it. Drea fussed at him for not having her back, but he was smart enough to know when to just shut the hell up.

"Nephewww... you got on them grey sweats for auntie don't ya?" Aunt Shirley appeared in the living room with her flask as soon as Mari spoke to Victoria and sat down on the couch.

"You done started already," Mari chuckled and shook his head.

"Started? When does she ever stop?" Victoria huffed.

"Don't start Vicky... Ima tell the girls bout their new daddy if you..."

"Shirley shut the hell up!"

"Mama why you in here cussin?" Drea emerged from the kitchen.

"If you think that's cussin, baby you ain't seen shit. Sis been showing her ass ever since... shit! If you didn't have that baby I would get up and slap yo ass!" Aunt Shirley cut her story off and threatened her sister when she was hit with the remote control.

"Come try this baby," Drea pulled Mari up and he followed her into the kitchen.

"What you want me to try?" he quizzed.

"Nothin really. I just wanted a kiss," she pulled him in and slid her tongue in his mouth once he leaned down a little.

"Oh so you ain't mad a nigga no mo huh... you want me to take you in the bedroom and break you off?" he smacked her on the ass.

"Leave the past in the past," she kissed him again.

"Cut that shit out in this kitchen. My man ain't here so hell yeah I'm cock blocking. Drea yo ass gon end up pregnant again. Probably already pregnant. I told Lexi that when she said you was having mood swings and shit," Aunt Shirley rattled on.

"Lexi still tell you every damn thang huh. Y'all two get on my damn nerves," Drea hissed.

"Drea don't be in here talking bout Sexi Lexi. I can hear," Lexi made a dramatic entrance like she always did with J.R. right behind her.

Mari went and dapped him up and was ready to leave the women in the kitchen.

"You still telling Auntie everything. I thought y'all only did that when y'all smoke," Drea sassed.

"You need to hurry up and have Shirley Junior so we can smoke," Shirley said.

"Shirley Junior. I know you ain't thought my sister was naming her baby no Shirley Junior," Anastasia walked in.

"Don't y'all lil Holiday hoes try to gang up on me now. I'm still y'all elder and I'll whoop all y'all asses," Aunt Shirley fussed.

"Where Mani?" Mari asked Anastasia.

"Fuck yo brother," Stasia rolled her eyes and Mari hated that he even asked.

The two of them had been going through a rough patch, but he knew that his brother loved the hell out of Anastasia. He hoped that they could work their relationship out, but he knew his brother well enough to know that he damn sure wasn't gonna beg for long.

A few minutes later, Mari's phone started vibrating on the

counter. Drea picked it up and handed it to him and it was his brother calling.

"What up?"

"Yo come help me get these drinks and shit," Mani said and hung up before he could respond.

"Let me go help Mani right quick," Mari excused himself.

It wasn't too cold outside, so he didn't bother putting a jacket on. As soon as he opened the door, he came face to face with his mom who was holding what he knew had to be a caramel cake. She had made a few other dishes to add onto dinner, but Mari had requested his favorite dessert and knew that she would come through.

"Hey ma," he kissed her on the cheek.

"Hey there son... that brother of yours driving me insane. I'll be glad when Anastasia take him back," Linda rolled her eyes and Mari laughed.

With her mouth, mixed with Aunt Shirley's he knew the day was about to be crazy as fuck. Mari went and helped his brother and after two trips, they were done and back chillin in the house. Just when he was about to cut a piece of cake, his mom walked up and smacked the shit out of his hand.

"Shit... I mean shoot ma."

"No sweets before dinner. It don't matter who house we at, you know the rules," Linda fussed.

"Heeyyy everybody," Lyssa's voice could be heard before she made it to the kitchen and Mari knew that Corey was with her. He had been granted a pass for the day so everyone was together.

"Uh oh... hide ya purses and wallets. The crackhead is here y'all," Shirley announced.

"My husband is not a crackhead Aunt Shirley," Alyssa bellowed.

"Baby, people who steal, kill, drink, and pop pills are all

crackheads, Ion care how you try to dress it up," Shirley countered.

"Ain't that what you said..."

"Auntie come on let's go outside," Lexi drug her out of the kitchen.

"Come on guys. Let's go to the man cave until it's time to eat.

"D'Mari," he heard Drea call out to him.

When he turned around she was holding his phone and the look she had on her face wasn't a good one.

"Who the hell is this?" she asked and handed him his phone.

Mari stared at the text message in disbelief while Drea's eyes pierced a hole through his soul.

27

As the men sat in the man cave talking shit and drinking, it felt like old times for Corey. Being at the rehab away from his family was starting to fuck with his mental. After Alyssa threatened the entire staff to let him come home for the holiday, it didn't surprise him when his shrink came to him granting him permission to go home for the day. Even though he put on a brave front, Corey needed to be home with his family. Although Corey was enjoying spending time with his family, he knew that he was under scrutiny. With plenty of alcohol and drugs floating around the house, he viewed his surroundings as a test and Corey was determined not to break.

Listening to his brothers talk about the problems they were having with their women made him realize how much they weren't telling him when they came to visit him. Corey understood that his family didn't want to concern him with their problems but he didn't want to be iced out altogether and learning about the shit that was going on in the streets really fucked him up. Corey listened carefully as they filled him in on all the shit that had been going down since he'd been away and the news had on him on a hundred but the fact that his brothers seemed to have a handle on shit eased his mind a little.

"So, what's been new with you C? You finally started woosha-ing with the junkies in the rehab?" J.R. poured another round of Henny for everyone except him.

"I guess you can say that. Between Alyssa and the psychologist, they kinda gave me no choice. If I didn't start talking, they're gonna keep my ass in there even longer and if that shit happened, Alyssa threatened to chop my dick off so she could still have sex without cheating," Corey chuckled.

"Damn!" they all responded in unison.

"That's some straight savage shit," D'Mani shook his head before taking a sip of his drink.

"Speaking of coming home, did they give you a release date yet?" D'Mani asked.

"Fuck no but hopefully I gained some brownie points for being a willing participant in the meetings because I'm ready to get out of that motherfucker like yesterday."

"I hear that."

"So listen y'all... I got drop another mufuckin bomb all y'all," J.R. announced and the room got silent.

"What up man?" Mari finally asked when J.R. didn't continue.

"Long story short, my sister was goin through my OG shit and y'all won't believe the last name that was on my birth certificate..."

Before anyone could say another word, there was a knock on the door.

"The food is done y'all. Come eat," Lexi said as she opened the door.

"Aight bae. Here we come," J.R responded and let the guys know that they would continue the conversation later since Lexi's nosey ass didn't leave.

The men headed out of the man cave and down to the dining room where the table was decorated with plates, silverware, delicious food and desserts. Corey's stomach began to growl at the sight of the spread and instantly found a seat next his wife. Corey glanced around the table and could feel the tension between the twins and their women and hoped that they could put their differences to the side so they wouldn't fuck up the family dinner. When everyone was seated, Victoria stood up to bless the food.

"Aight Vicky, don't say no long ass blessing. Keep it short and sweet now," Aunt Shirley huffed.

"Well if you shut up, I can start," Victoria glared at her sister. "Dear heavenly father, we thank you for allowing us to see another day and allowing all our of family to be here for this special occasion. Bless the people at this table as well as the food that we're about to eat. In Jesus name we pray, Amen."

"Amen," the family said in unison.

Everyone at the table began to fill their plates up with turkey, ham, dressing, potato salad, collard greens, string beans, devil eggs and other delicious sides. When he finished preparing his plate, Corey didn't hesitate to dig in.

"Damn boy! Slow down over there," Linda gasped at her nephew. "Ya ass didn't just come home from doing a bid," everyone laughed.

"Leave that boy alone Linda. You know his ass is detoxing all that shit outta his system. Let the crackhead enjoy his food. He's looking a lil skinny over there," Aunt Shirley chimed in.

The table burst into laughter including Corey. He wanted to speak up in his defense, but he was trying not to choke on his food.

"Y'all not gonna be coming for my husband now," Alyssa spoke up for her man with a smirk on her face.

"Let my son in law eat in peace. It ain't like a certain somebody at this table don't need to be in rehab herself," Victoria shot causing everyone's eyes to look in Aunt Shirley's direction.

"Fuck all y'all," she glared.

The table erupted in laughter once more as they continued to eat their food. Although he was the center of most of the jokes that afternoon, Corey wasn't offended at all. He knew how his family rolled and knew that he had it coming. What started out as depressing situation for him, Corey had finally got to a place where he could laugh the shit off without feeling salty. At times, he felt like he wasn't making any progress but being around his family made him realize that he was making more progress than he thought.

After an afternoon of laughs and sports, Corey was reluctant to leave but he knew he had to. He said his good-byes to the family and lingered around a little longer than he was supposed to before getting into Alyssa's ride and heading back to rehab. The sight of the center irritated his soul but Corey knew what time it was. He let out a long sigh when she put the car in park.

"I know you didn't wanna leave the fam bae but just think. Hopefully in a few months, this place will be a thing of the past," Alyssa smiled.

"I know, baby," he sighed.

Corey wrapped his arms around his wife embracing her tightly.

"I wanna thank you for standing by me through all of this. You don't know how much that shit means to me Lyssa," he spoke into her ear.

"I'll always be here for you Corey. For better or worse. I just hope you'll always be here too."

Caught off guard by her words, he hugged her a little as he wondered what his wife meant by the statement she made.

Kissing her passionately, Corey hopped out the car and stood on the curb until Alyssa was out of sight. As he headed inside the building, he signed himself back in then headed down the hallway to his room. He stopped by Larry's room to see what was up with him but when he saw that he had company, Corey walked away. Stopping in mid step, he leaned back to get a better glimpse of the woman he was talking to. He didn't know why the female looked familiar to him but the longer he stared at her, the vibe he got just from looking at her caused the sirens to go off in his head.

❧ 28 ❧

D'Mani still hadn't talked to Stasia and he wasn't sure
how he felt about it. On the one hand, it had been
pretty peaceful for him and on the other he missed
his little homie Kyler and even her aggravating ass. He had
never pictured that Anastasia would act the way that she had
been since finding out about Imani. She was making it difficult for him to keep defending her to even Cheyanne, not
that she was the topic of their conversations, just in general.

It was seeming more and more like the confidence that
had attracted him in the first place was gone now and he
could understand how his situation could partially be to
blame. The thing was though that he hadn't cheated on her to
make Imani, and besides the history that him and Cheyanne
shared there was no reason for her to feel like she had to
compete. Women were weird like that though, but he
couldn't lie and say that he wasn't ready to go back home. Not
being able to spend the holiday with his family wasn't something that he liked and although he had his mama and Imani
it wasn't complete without Anastasia and Kyler. Maybe

instead of giving her the space she asked for he should've been fighting to keep his family together.

With that thought in mind D'Mani was up and in his car heading to Tiffany's. Although with her settlement Anastasia didn't need or want for anything, a big part of what kept her happy before was him surprising her with gifts. With all of the shit going on in their lives like moving, starting up their empire in Atlanta, the beef they had with Tessa and Imani thrown into the mix he had fallen off and that probably made it easier for her to feel insecure in her spot. That he could admit fault for and he was about to start trying to make it up to her.

D'Mani walked inside of the Phipps Plaza and headed straight to the Tiffany store first. As soon as he walked in two of the workers spotted him and speed walked in his direction. He was sure that it had everything to do with the Audemars Piguet that shined on his wrist, because the light gray joggers and black tee and Jordan's he was wearing didn't give away his wealth. The blonde ended up stopping in front of him first and he could see the disappointed look on the other girl's face as she fell back and went back to her spot behind the counter.

"Good morning, is there anything I can help you find today?" the blonde whose name tag read Becky smiled showing all of her teeth. D'Mani smirked at the irony of running into a "becky with good hair", before replying.

"Uh, yeah. I'm lookin for somethin nice to get my girl, I'm not sure what I should get though."

"Wellllll, I guess it would depend. What's the occasion... anniversary? engagement? Or are you in the dog house?" she asked lowering her voice like somebody else might hear when she got to the last part. D'Mani didn't really like how she asked him about being in the "doghouse", but that was precisely the reason he was there.

"Uhhhh, that last one." He coughed, uncomfortable admitting that.

"Oh well that's alright! You'd be surprised how many men have to come in and buy their way back into their wives or girlfriend's good graces. Let's look over here, these are what I like to call the "please forgive me" pieces." She chuckled and led him over to the counter on the right where there was a display of diamond earrings, necklaces, bracelets and rings. The selection was a little overwhelming to him considering that it was rare that he had to buy something to express an apology. He looked over each piece until his eyes landed on a diamond necklace, with matching diamond stud earrings. Pointing it out to Becky, he had her remove it from the display so that he could get a closer look. The diamonds in both pieces shined and showed a perfect resolution. It was no doubt in his mind that she was going to love them.

"I'll take these right here. I think she'll like it." He said firmly still looking down into the display to make sure he didn't want anything else.

"Heck she better! This is gorgeous, I'd just melt if a man got me anything like this." Becky cooed forcing him to look up at her. D'Mani didn't miss the look of lust in her eyes, but he wasn't biting. Nothing against them, but he just wasn't attracted to white women. As far as he was concerned black women were lit and there was nothing that a white girl could do for him with her pancake booty having ass.

"You might actually get a man too if you stopped flirtin with taken ones." He told her coldly. She gasped and started opening and closing her mouth like she was unsure of how to respond.

"I...uh...I wasn't, trying to imply anything." She stuttered looking uncomfortable all of a sudden.

"Good, cause all I need you to do is bag this and then ring it up for me. Think you can handle that without comin out yo body?" she nodded without speaking period and told him to meet her at the register.

By the time she had finished bagging up his stuff and made it to where he stood waiting her professionalism was back and after paying the fifteen thousand for his gift he left the store in search of some flowers. He was going to wine and dine his way back into Stasia's life if it was the last thing he did.

About two hours later he was on his way to him and Stasia's home with three dozen red roses, and the Tiffany bag in the passenger seat. Though he wished he could have put more planning into it, he knew that he had to work with what he had. Besides it wasn't like he could be sure of Anastasia's location, and it would have been fucked up to have dinner or something scheduled for them and then she was MIA.

When he finally pulled up to her house he saw her car pulling into the garage and then the door coming back down, so his timing was perfect. He gave her a few minutes to get settled inside before grabbing up the flowers and the blue bag she loved so much, and making his way up to the door. Standing there ringing the doorbell to the house they once shared irritated him a little bit, but he tried not to let it show the sudden need for a blunt passed through him. D'Mani couldn't lie, he was a little nervous considering how Stasia had been acting as of late. He hesitated for a second before ringing the doorbell a second time. It wasn't long before Anastasia came to the door and upon seeing him standing there a frown marred her face.

"What are you doin here D'Mani?" was the first thing out of her mouth and it was like the words got stuck in his throat. He couldn't say that he was expecting a warm greeting or anything, but he figured once she saw the roses and bag she would at least smile. Even as her eyes scanned over the gifts though her face still showed displeasure, and he for damn sure wasn't expecting that.

"I came over to apologize for how things been goin, I don't like this rough patch we goin through and so I figured that I would take the first step in making things right." He finally said once he'd found his voice. She didn't say anything right away. It seemed like she was considering what he'd said, but when tears sprang to her eyes and she shook her head emphatically D'Mani knew that it wasn't going to be as easy as he thought.

"It's a little too late for this D'Mani! You made me feel second best when you know I've already been through that before."

D'Mani tried to think of a single time where he'd made her feel like her dead ex-husband, but kept coming up short. He thought that maybe she was just being dramatic with the way that she was acting, but she really did think that he had done something wrong to her, and now she was legit playing him like a bitch!

"Quit fuckin playin with me Stasia! You done for real took this shit too far already." He snapped, unable to control the anger he was feeling. He threw the flowers on the ground, and crumpled the bag in his hands, but what he really wanted to do was beat her ass over the head with them expensive ass roses, especially when she stood there and laughed.

"No nigga! I ain't took it far enough! But I'm bout to though." She smirked wickedly and D'Mani took a step back to put some more distance between them, because it was no telling what was about to come out of her mouth.

"Anastasia." His voice came out in a warning tone. "Watch what the fuck you let come out yo mouth Ma. I ain't that fuck ass nigga Richard or Zyree-."

"Nah you worse! Came along making me think shit is

going to be good, then you pop up with a baby! You spendin nights at that bitch house-!"

"That was one fuckin night-!"

"So, it shouldn't have happened once! Then you had the nerve to take my son over there! As far as I'm concerned, we done, done nigga, and I'ma show you just how serious I am!" As if on cue D'Mani heard a male voice call out "baby" from inside.

"Here I come!" she hollered back before slamming the door shut right in his face. He had been so close to snatching her ass out there with him, but her sneaky ass was too quick.

"Stasia I swear to God it bet not be no nigga in there! Open this fuckin door!" he growled pounding his fist against the wood. All he could see was red. All this time he had been being faithful and only doing what he was supposed to just for her to have some nigga in his house! He never would have disrespected her like that no matter what she had done. D'Mani realized that the problem was he always handled her with kiddie gloves, he never really had a reason to show out on her before, but that shit was over! He began to kick at the door and the sound of the wood splitting made him go harder.

"Oh my God D'Mani what the hell are you doin!" Stasia screamed from somewhere in the house, but by then he'd already gotten it open enough for him to step inside. His eyes quickly scanned the foyer looking for whatever nigga was about to be wheeled out of there but all he saw was Anastasia standing next to the stairs with the phone in her hand.

"Where the fuck he at Stasia? Huh!" he asked, but she was frozen in fear and shaking like a leaf. D'Mani saw a flash of color run past the dining room and took off catching whoever he was right as he got to the door that led to the garage. He quickly tackled him to the floor and landed a barrage of punches to the nigga face while Anastasia cried and screamed in the background. By the time D'Mani had finished with him he couldn't even make out the features on dude's face and the tight ass blue, polo shirt he wore was covered in blood. Still breathing heavily he backed away to where Stasia stood crying next to the refrigerator.

"Yo ass tryna leave me for another Richard ass nigga?" he frowned at the slacks and penny loafers the nigga was wearing before turning back to her. "I did everything right. I ain't lie to you and I damn sure ain't cheat on you! All a nigga guilty of is getting somebody pregnant BEFORE I even met yo ass, but you can have that Ma! I hope you enjoy bein a nurse cause that nigga gone be sippin through a straw for the next few months."

He didn't even wait for her to try and get out another word, he was done with her ass. His only regret was not being sure if Kyler was home or not, but it was too late to worry about that. She had done more than crossed the line, she had played hopscotch on that bitch, but he was gone be the one with the last laugh. She could bet that.

29

A couple of weeks had passed since D'Mani had stomped that nigga out in Stasia's kitchen, and he still didn't have any remorse. He was guessing that she must have come to her senses because she had started to blow his phone up immediately once he left, but he blocked her ass. When he said he wasn't fucking with her he hadn't been lying. He wasn't about to play that back and forth shit with her, especially over something so petty. D'Mani planned to get it all off of his mind though because it was his baby girl's birthday, and he couldn't wait to see the look on her face when she saw the pink baby Mercedes pull up. He couldn't stop smiling and thinking about all the fun she was going to have that day, and how he'd be able to finally celebrate with her.

Since she wasn't a fan of over extravagant parties Cheyanne had decided to throw the party at her house with a few of her friends and some family members. D'Mani pulled up outside to see that the driveway and street were full of cars. He didn't have to look too far for a parking spot. Once he was parked he walked the short distance to the house and rang the bell.

Imani opened the door looking extremely cute in a pair of Minnie Mouse Chuck Taylor's, some dark blue jean capris and an airbrushed shirt that had the same character and the words birthday girl scrawled across the back. He knew that because he had helped Cheyanne pick it out. Things between them had been just as good as they had always been, but better since Stasia wasn't wreaking havoc on their co-parenting relationship.

"Hey Daddy! It's my birthday!" she shouted and jumped into his arms giving him a tight hug.

"Girl, I know that, you only been talkin about it every day for the last month." He chuckled planting a kiss on her chubby cheek.

"Wellllll, somebody had to remind you." She told him sassily, then began to look around him. "where Kyler?"

He was afraid that she would ask him that, and he didn't have an answer for her. The truth was the last time he had seen his little homie was the day they'd gone out to eat and he had to cut it short. He was hoping that with all of the excitement from the party she wouldn't think to ask, but they had bonded and she considered him like a cool big brother.

"Where *is* Kyler Imani, and didn't I tell you not to answer this door lil girl? You let a grown up get it." Cheyanne walked up fussing and looking sexy as hell in a yellow sundress, but smiled once she saw D'Mani standing there.

"Only people for my party comin Ma." Imani told her matter of factly.

"Whatever lil girl, don't do that mess no more." She warned pointing at her nose playfully, but there was still a serious undertone to her words.

"Aye, listen to yo mama." D'Mani chimed in and sat her back down on the floor.

"Okay." She whined before running off and joining a group of screaming girls.

"Thanks." Cheyanne breathed with a smile still covering her beautiful face.

"No problem."

"Well come on let me introduce you to everybody." She told him turning around so that her ass was on full display. It had been a hot minute since D'Mani had slid up in some pussy and he couldn't deny that the longer he went without it the more Cheyanne was looking like a full meal. He was trying to keep their relationship on a platonic level, but it was becoming hard not to give in to temptation. She stopped in the living room and reintroduced him to her mother and two sisters, before walking him around the room so that he could meet everybody who had anything to do with Imani.

By the time he'd been introduced to everyone in the room they were screaming for cake and ice cream. He helped her make out the plates for the kids after they blew out the candles and then he went to set up her presents on the table outside where they all were supposed to be sitting when baby girl started opening her presents. D'Mani snuck out and got the car out so that it would be waiting when Imani finished eating.

By the time the gifts were set on the table the way that Cheyanne wanted D'Mani was surprised to see that the kids were all done eating and back outside. He had barely had time to sit down and drink the beer that Cheyanne had given him. It wasn't a big deal though, he was happy to be at Imani's beck and call. So when she ran out demanding that he play with her and her friends he didn't deny her, he got his grown ass up and ran around with kids in Cheyanne's big backyard that was full of balls, balloons, a kiddie pool and a bouncy house. While they were running around he noticed Cheyanne watching them with a content look on her face. He tried hard not to stare back at her, but it was like their eyes were drawn to each other. They gave each other the eye pretty much the whole party and when it was over, and the guests were all gone he offered to stay and help her clean up the mess. Imani had partied until she fell out on the floor in the living room and D'Mani worked around her picking up any garbage that was laying around, while Cheyanne cleaned the kitchen.

"So how was your first birthday party with the princess?"

D'Mani turned to see Cheyanne standing leaned up against the doorway of the living room with an amused smirk.

"Uhhh, it was ayite. As long as I got to see baby girl open up her presents and have fun I'm happy." He shrugged. She nodded that she understood and the two stood there in silence for a second.

"Well you wanna come have another drink?" she asked in a low tone.

"Hell yeah I low key need one after all this excitement." They both chuckled.

"Okay come on. Do you want a beer or something a little stronger?" she questioned as I followed her into the kitchen.

"Do you even gotta ask?"

"Right. Let me get the shot glasses." She went into a cabinet by the sink and pulled out two glasses and grabbed one of the bottles of Patron from the counter, that he'd seen her making margaritas with throughout the day.

"Do you think you should even have any more of this?" he teased and she gasped in fake shock before clutching her chest.

"Nigga I does this." She rolled her eyes hard and poured a hefty amount into each glass.

"Yeah ayite don't be tryna pass out on me, I know how yo ass is when you been drinkin. You can barely handle one cup let alone all the ones I done seen you chug today. Shit, I'm surprised you still standin."

"Let you tell it nigga. You was the one who couldn't hold yo liquor. Every time you got drunk all yo' ass wanted to do was fuck and go to sleep." She laughed and downed the liquor in her glass then poured another.

"Shit, that much ain't changed." D'Mani thought that he had said that in his head, but from the look on her face he knew that it had really slipped out. Cheyanne swallowed hard and he could see her breathing pick up. "my bad I ain't mean to say that out loud." He admitted pouring himself another shot and swallowing it down.

"I figured that," she said unable to meet his gaze. A silence fell over them once again and D'Mani licked his lips as he looked over her body since they were sitting next to each other at the island he had the perfect view of her ass.

"Come ere' girl." He ordered biting into his bottom lip. Her face registered shock and she shook her head quickly climbing down from off the stool and backing away.

"I think we done had a lil too much." She went to turn her back on him and he was behind her in seconds with his chest pressed against her back. He felt her body stiffen up, but relaxed her with a kiss to the back of her neck. She had always liked that. "D'Mani.... we shouldn't." she moaned and a shudder rippled through her body.

"Tell me you don't want it, and I'll leave." He said still planting kisses along her neck and ear, while his hands slipped underneath her dress. She didn't stop him from dipping a finger into her wetness and that let him know that the feelings he had were mutual.

"Ahhhhhh." She threw her head back onto his shoulder as he rubbed her clit between his fingers and stuck his tongue in her ear. D'Mani could feel her juices dripping down his fingers and his dick got harder than it already was, straining against the fabric of his jeans.

"Got damnn." He huffed as she began to grind against his hand. At that point he knew she wanted the dick, but he asked anyway. "you want me to stop?" his voice came out husky.

"No, mmmm shit I'ma come D'Mani." She whined quietly and he decided to put her out of her misery. Bending her over the counter he snatched away the white thong she wore and shoved himself inside of her in one swift motion. Cheyanne's pussy was just how he remembered it, wet and tight and he had to wait a second before he could move just from the feel of it. She must have been backed up too because she stiffened up like she couldn't handle it.

"Loosen the fuck up Chey! Don't tell me you can't handle this dick no more." He growled taking a handful of her hair and pulling it back.

"Yesss, yess I can take it!"

"Then show me, show out on this shit," that was all he had to say and Cheyanne began throwing it back on him just like old times. He eventually took over and started delivering deep strokes as he watched her pussy soak his dick up. "damn girl!" seeing how wet she was and how much of her juice was dripping down his shaft D'Mani was finding it hard to hold on. He could feel his nut beginning to rise as she contracted around him sucking him all the way in and before he could stop himself he'd spilled his seeds inside of her. Gripping her waist tighter he rode the wave of his orgasm. When his dick finally stopped pulsing inside of her they both seized their movement and just sat in the same position with him still inside of her as they caught their breath.

Cheyanne was the first one to move away and her face was full of guilt as she paced back and forth while he grabbed some paper towels to clean himself off. "Oh my god this was a mistake!" she groaned with one hand against her forehead and the other planted on her hips.

"You damn right it was a mistake bitch!" He turned to see Anastasia standing there with a present in her hand and knew it was about to be some shit.

🙐 30 🙒

Since Thanksgiving, Corey had been more determined than ever to get out of the hell hole that he'd called home for the past couple of months. Every day, someone was dragging someone new into the facility and each person seemed to be worse than the last. Corey was growing tired of hearing the screams of the fiends that would be coming down from their highs. It was starting to aggravate the fuck out of him and was beginning to fuck *with* him. So to keep his mind right, Corey exercised. No matter what time of day it was.

Besides steering clear of the junkies, Corey's relationship with Larry seemed to be going better than expected. Over the short period of the time they'd known each other, he discovered that they had a few things in common in their personal and family lives. Whenever they would have a conversation pertaining to a personal matter, they kept the conversation limited and didn't reveal any names. By the way that Larry talked, Corey knew that he was involved in the streets in one form or another. Corey figured if he remained patient, things would begin to unfold soon enough.

It was the middle of the week and Corey wanted to jump for joy when one of the nurses informed him that the group meeting was canceled for the day. With nothing on his schedule, he decided to chill and watch a few movies on Netflix. As he watched Friday, one of his favorite movies, the knock on the door caused his eyes to shift from his phone to the person interrupting his movie. When he saw that it was Deana, the aide, Corey gave her a small smile and sat up in his bed.

"Wassup with you?"

"Nothing much," she blushed. "I'm about to run to the store to get something to eat and wanted to know if you wanted me to bring you back anything."

"Deana, don't take what I'm about to say to you the wrong way, but why do you always ask me do I need anything whenever you work?" Corey questioned.

The smile on her face seemed to vanish as her eyes shifted to the floor.

"I mean, I'm almost positive that you'll get in trouble if someone caught you sneaking me food or anything else."

"I know I've been offering to get you food since you've been in here and I'm sure that you already know this but...I'm *attracted* to you. I know you got wife and everything and I don't want to mess that up. I just want to be useful to you in any way while you're here," she confessed.

Corey took a moment to let Deana's words sink in and figure out if he wanted to use her to his advantage. Deana looked to be a few years younger than him, and although he only seen her in her uniform, Corey could tell that she was working with a bomb ass body. But *fucking her* wasn't on his mind at all but using her to be his eyes and ears on the outside was what he really wanted her for. Since learning about all the shit that had been going on with his brothers, Corey needed to find out if all this shit was being done by one person or if the niggas that shot him were gunning for his family in his place. Whatever the situation was, Corey needed answers soon. Instead of having Deana start right away with gathering information, he figured he would start her off with a few easy assignments, give her a few compliments, and then toss her ass to the wolves.

"Okay Deana. I'll take you up on your offer," he smiled.

"Really?"

"Yeah. If you won't tell, I won't tell."

"That works for me. So, what can I get you?"

Corey told her to bring him a party box from Taco Bell and one liter Pepsi. Deana gave him a big smile before she dashed out his room and down the hall. Nodding his head in satisfaction, Corey went back to watching his movie.

When his movie came to an end, Corey searched for a new one when the sound of yelling came from down the hall. Like everyone else in the building, he went to go see what was going on, and when he saw that it was Larry, Corey walked down the hell to see what was up.

"What's going on, bro?"

"I got a little bit of bad news a few minutes ago, but I'll deal with that shit later," Larry sighed before sitting down on his bed.

The room fell silent as Corey walked further into the room.

"My sister just told me that some nigga she fucking with keep putting his hands on her and shit. I keep telling her dumb ass to ditch that bitch ass nigga but she never does. I swear she act like a young dumb bitch instead of a woman that's about to be in her thirties," Larry shook his head.

"Don't let that shit stress you, man. You just gotta let her outgrow the nigga on her own. It ain't shit you can do about it until she decides to leave on her own."

"See, that's where you're wrong because as soon as I'm up out this bitch, I'm on his ass. That motherfucka done took too much from me already. I gave this nigga my sister and he abuses her. His days are the fuck number. You can believe that shit, youngin'," Larry pointed at him.

Corey nodded his head in understanding and couldn't help but wonder who Larry was talking about. The two men chopped it up for a little while longer before a call came through on Larry's phone and Corey stepped out the room.

As he walked back down the hall to his room, Corey spotted Janice and Deana having what seemed to be like a heated conversation based off their body language. When Corey walked passed them, their conversation came to a halt and he felt their eyes on him until he dipped into his room. The thought of Deana talking to Janice put a bad taste in his mouth. Janice was a slick bitch. She tried to make nice with everyone to get in their business, and once she had some dirt on you, no matter what it was, she used it to her advantage to blackmail people into doing whatever she wanted. Whenever Janice glanced his way, Corey ignored her ass and kept it pushing. He never saw Deana and Janice interact since he'd been there and wanted to know what was being discussed.

"Hey Corey, here's your food. I had to hide it in my duffle bag from nosey ass Janice," Deana rolled her eyes.

"I appreciate this, Deana."

"No problem. I was happy to do it."

"Is everything cool with you and Janice?"

"Yeah. She was just scolding me for coming back late from my break. Nothing for you to worry about it," she confirmed.

"And if there was something I needed to worry about?"

"I'll tell you right away," Deana winked. "Well, I gotta get back to work. Call me if you need me."

Corey didn't know if Deana was telling the truth or not, but since he didn't have a reason to doubt her, he let it go. The smell of the food caught his attention and his stomach growled. Stashing the food in his nightstand drawer, Corey headed to the restroom to wash his hands. Drying his hands with a few paper towels, he tossed them in the trash and left out but stopped in his tracks when he heard someone in the stairway mentioned D'Mani's name. Peeking through the glass window, Corey saw Janice talking to the woman that was there to see Larry on Thanksgiving. Only staying in the window for a few seconds, he strolled down the hall as if nothing happened, but when he got in his room, he closed the door behind and was ready to destroy his whole room. But instead, he just paced the floor. Corey's blood level was through the fucking roof as he thought about why Janice and the bitch of Larry's had his brother's name in their mouths. Being as though it was Larry's bitch in the stairway talking to Janice, it made him feel like that she was the one doing his dirty work and Janice was on their team.

Although shit seemed so clear to Corey, he couldn't make any moves until he knew for sure what the fuck was going on and the rolled that everyone played. He made a mental note to sleep with one eye open for the remainder of his stay at the rehab.

𝓢 31 𝓢

POW!

J.R. reached back as far as he could, landing a hard blow to the side of her face before cocking his gun and aiming it at her head.

"I'm not playing *no* more games with you. Either you gon' tell me what I want to hear or I'm shooting off a body part, starting with your legs... now how are you connected to Tessa?" he screamed, spit flying from his mouth.

"Fuck you!" she spit at him, showing no fear whatsoever.

J.R. laughed before stepping back, avoiding her bodily fluids. As promised, he pulled the trigger, sending a hot bullet through her right leg. Although she was a stuff cookie to crack, baby girl must had a low tolerance for pain because she screamed out in pain.

"Ohhhh, the bullet not your friend huh? You better talk," he urged her.

"You gon' have to kill me," she cried.

Taking that as an invitation to add more bullets to her body, J.R. shot her in the other leg, getting the same reaction he got before. He knew her type, she was a *real* bitch, but he knew that even the realest folded at times.

168

"Ok look Jessica....." he started and paused, capturing her reaction to being called by her name.

"Jessica Sanchez right? 2358 Washington Street, Apartment 2E right?" he paused again.

Jessica's eyes grew the sized of golf balls, a visible lump formed in her throat.

"You got triplets right? Three girls actually and they attend Chapel Hill Middle School in Douglas County right? Bitch, I know you ain't think that we just had you down here and not doing our research," he stated.

"You hurt my babies and I'll....."

"Ahhhhh shut up bitch, you ain't gon' do shit. As a matter of fact, you can't do shit. But I'll tell you what... if you talk, tell me what I need to hear, then they'll arrive home safe today; if not, then.... well you know," he chuckled.

"YOU FUCK'N' BITCH. TOUCH THEM AND I SWEAR YOU ARE A DEAD MAN!" she screamed.

"Wait... I ain't done. I did a little more research and come to find out that Tessa is their father but you *not* a wife. Therefore, that makes you this *dumb* down ass *side bitch* who the nigga don't really give two fucks about because if he did, you'll be protected like his wife and other kids. But noooooo.... You just some *fake* ride or die ass bitch who he can give two fucks about," J.R. explained.

Judging by her body language, J.R. knew he hit the nail right on the head, so he kept going.

"Look shorty, you tell me where I can find them and you free to go," he lied.

"If I tell you then we both dead," Jessica finally spoke with some sense.

"Nah, you got my word and I'm a man of my word."

J.R. stared into her eyes, hoping she was buying the bullshit he was selling, but he wasn't sure.

"Ok look. We can get to all the technical shit later, just

answer me this one question. I know Tessa's cartel consist of brothers but tell me more about Justin," he suggested.

"Jus---Justin?" she repeated back slowly.

"How you know about Justin?" Jessica continued.

"I'm asking the questions, remember?" J.R. reminded her.

Jessica stared at J.R., squinting her eyes as if she was trying to figure it out.

"You---yo—you look just like him," she smiled, showcasing a perfect set of teeth.

The mood had completely changed in the dark damp room they were in.

"You Kenya's son.... OH MY GOD! It all makes sense now!" Jessica exclaimed.

Jessica's whole persona changed. She went from this ruthless bitch to having a soft spot for what reason, J.R. had no clue.

"How the fuck do you know my mom?" he quizzed, cocking his pistol again and aiming it at her.

Fed up with the bullshit and the fact that he was more confused than before, J.R. was ready to kill the bitch and get it over with.

"Listen to me..... Tessa's cartel is *not* to be fucked with. You need to check on your family ASAP. I am your last concern," she warned him.

"What?" he asked with a screwed face.

"CHECK ON YO FUCK'N' FAMILY NOW!" she yelled.

It was something about the tone of her voice that let J.R. know she was not bullshitting. He grabbed his phone and called Lexi, but she didn't answer. He called their house phone, along with Yasmine's cell and still no answer. Without acknowledging Jessica any more, J.R. ran out and did the dash to his house. He called D'Mani to tell him to check on them, but he didn't answer either.

What usually was a thirty-minute drive, J.R. chopped it in half. When he pulled up, he noticed extra cars on his block, but he shrugged it off. He pulled into the driveway behind Lexi's car and jumped out before the car stopped completely. J.R. sprinted across their manicured lawn and to the front door. He fumbled with his keys, even dropping them twice before he finally got it together. Once he opened the front door, his mouth dropped opened as everyone yelled "SURPRISE!"

J.R. glanced around his home, which was decorated with balloons and other decorations. It wasn't his birthday, so he was clueless as to what the celebration about.

"Baby look what they did for us!" Alexis walked over to him smiling, hugging him.

"With all the shit we been going through, them damn Holiday sisters thought it'll be cool to surprise y'all with a gender reveal party," Mari walked up and stated.

"Why you ain't answer yo phone?" he turned to Lexi and asked.

"It's on the charger. Ain't you happy?" she gushed.

"Where's Yasmine?" he asked to no one in particular.

"She left this morning to register for school, what's wrong?" Lexi replied.

J.R. grabbed his phone and called his little sister but got no answer. He dialed her back to back and again, got the voicemail. Just as he was about to flip, a text message came through from her.

Yasmine: I'm at the door.

J.R. let out a long sigh. To say he was relieved would be an understatement. He needed to know exactly why Jessica warned him. He planned on getting to the bottom of things that day. Loosening up a little, J.R. walked to the door to open it for Yasmine because he had yet given her a key. When he got to the door, she wasn't on the porch yet, but a ring box sat on their welcome mat. J.R. bent down, retrieving the box while checking his surroundings and went back inside.

"Damn my nigga, you about to pop the big question?" D'Mani asked, noticing the jewelry box in his hand.

Instead of verbally acknowledging what he said, J.R. shook his head *no* and began to open the box. After removing the top, the contents inside almost brought up the meal he had for breakfast. J.R. stared at the ring his mom gave Yasmine. Attached to the ring was a bloody finger... his little sister's *bloody* finger.

༺ 32 ༻

"**O**h my God!!" Drea screamed.

"Is that a finger? Lyssa shrieked.

"What the fuck?" Lexi seethed.

"What in the hell y'all got goin' on over here? I'm goin' back to Mississippi," Aunt Shirley added.

D'Mari instantly reached and made sure that piece was in place. He took control and grabbed Drea first.

"Take your sisters and auntie to the basement babe. Let us handle this," Mari instructed her.

"What's goi..."

"Andrea, take everyone to the basement now," he cut her off and told her in a firmer voice.

When Mari looked up, he saw that J.R. had already started ushering Lexi to the basement. Once the room was empty of the females, they were free to talk.

"I'M GON' KILL EVERY MUTHAFUCKA IN THE TESSA CARTEL!! THAT'S MY BABY SISTER!!" J.R. fumed.

"Calm down bro... you know we gotta think smart," Mari coaxed.

"NAH FUCK ALL THAT! ALL THEM NIGGAZ GOOD AS DEAD!" J.R. knocked the lamp off the table and it shattered.

"Let me call Mani and you call Julian," Mari instructed as he called his twin.

He called his brother back to back, all to no avail and then it hit him that he mentioned the birthday party. Mari figured that him and Stasia must have made up since she wasn't there with her sisters. Mari had yet to meet his little niece, but he would in due time.

"Julian on his way," J.R. said, bringing Mari out of his thoughts.

"Bet... we need to get the women out of here... but let's check all around the house first," Mari instructed.

"As soon as we get them safe, I'm goin' to kill that bitch Jessica. She just warned me before I made it. But since I can't touch them niggaz yet, she good as dead," J.R. seethed.

The two of them walked outside and went in opposite directions. It didn't take long before they met back at the front of the house, both stating that the premises were clear. Noise could be heard coming from in the house and moments later, the front door opened and the sisters followed by their aunt barged out.

"D'Mani got my sister fucked up. I don't know what he did yet, but Ima kick his ass for making my sister cry," Lexi screamed.

"Let's go Lexi," Drea yelled.

"I'm coming too. I loves me a good fight and y'all knows how to put it down," Aunt Shirley chimed in.

"Take y'all asses back in the got damn hou..."

Bratatat Bratatat Bratatat Bratatat Bratatat Bratatat Bratatat Bratatat

"GET DOWN!!! GET DOWN!!! GET DOWN!!!" Mari and J.R. yelled in unison and then started firing their weapons back. The ladies immediately tried to get out of harm's way, but since they were out in the front yard, there wasn't too many places to hide. Mari and J.R. continued shooting until their enemies drove away and out of sight. Out of breath and with adrenalines pumping, Mari and J.R. surveyed their surrounding until they heard the most unforgettable screams coming from behind them.

"NOOOOOO! NOOOOO! WHAT THE FUCK?? NOOOOOO!" Lexi's gut wrenching scream could be heard after the gunshots stopped.

"DREA!! AUNT SHIRLEY! NOOOOOO! NOOOOOO!" Lyssa joined in with the screaming as she came running out of the house as fast as she could.

"GET UP DREA... GET UP AUNT SHIREY!!" Lexi franticly screamed and that's when Mari and J.R. turned back towards the sisters, noticing that both women were lying on the ground and covered in blood.

"FUUUCCCKKKKK!!! FUUUCCCKKKKK!!! DREA BABY!! NOOOOOO! STAY WITH ME BABY!! DREA... DREA... FUUUCCCKKKKK!!!" Mari roared as he took off running and made his way to his wife. When Mari noticed that Drea wasn't moving, his heart instantly dropped.

TO BE CONTINUED...

Made in the USA
Middletown, DE
07 September 2021